CW00458462

Death of the Family

DEATH OF THE FAMILY

Sue George

HUTCHINSON

LONDON SYDNEY AUCKLAND JOHANNESBURG

© Sue George 1989

All rights reserved

This edition first published in 1989 by Hutchinson,
an imprint of Century Hutchinson Ltd, Brookmount
House, 62–65 Chandos Place, London WC2N 4NW

Century Hutchinson Australia (Pty) Ltd
89–91 Albion Street, Surry Hills, NSW 2010

Century Hutchinson New Zealand Limited
PO Box 40–086, Glenfield, Auckland 10, New Zealand

Century Hutchinson South Africa (Pty) Ltd
PO Box 377, Bergvlei, 2012 South Africa

British Library Cataloguing in Publication Data

George, Sue
  Death of the family.
  I. Title.
  823'.914 [F]

  ISBN 0–09–173844–X

Phototypeset by Input Typesetting Ltd, London

Printed and bound in Great Britain by
Anchor Brendon Ltd, Tiptree, Essex.

Time present and time past
Are both perhaps present in time future,
And time future contained in time past.

T. S. Eliot, *Four Quartets*, 'Burnt Norton'

THE PAST

White dress, lemon gauze, many people, all crowded together with so much jollity that bubbles float up into the air, so many adverts. A wedding. White. Snow-white.

Such a nice wedding, they all said, all these people seen together from this side, my side, of a fish-eye mirror. To me, their laughter sounds raucous, their bodies twisted. Just right for the happiest day of your life.

I must gain some perspective of this now that I'm in my chair distant, staring into the mirror. They, on the other hand, are all close together, squashed and, as I move away from the wall, more distorted.

Pauline and Ray had been going out together for a long time when they got married, and although she was thought a little young at eighteen, everything else was thought quite suitable. Of course, no-one stopped to consider any harder than that. I was so pleased that at last I would have a bedroom to myself that I almost forgot what was happening to her. Anyway, she'd been going on and on about marriage for as long as she'd known him – almost four years – the reason was a mystery to me. I'd watched them together all that time, and decided she was welcome to him.

But I was only sixteen then, and couldn't look at things through the protective distance of a mirror. Of course, because it is a mirror, I can see myself there, too. Younger, twisted also, distorted. God, how much better things are now.

The distortions I see in the mirror were there at the time, too. But I couldn't fathom them, because everyone else who bothered to look saw the happy couple truly content, everything as it should be. They looked in their mirrors and thought they were seeing what was really there.

As the car arrived, Pauline was sitting at the dressing table, staring bleakly at herself in the mirror. She was wearing a frothy dress, cut high under the bust to make her look thinner, and an off-the-face headdress, to suit her round face and pale, fluffy hair. Viv thought she looked unusually pretty. Spread out on the table top was a random assortment of cosmetics, many of them borrowed.

'What shall I put on my face?' she said helplessly.

Viv was sitting on the bed, completely ready in her lemon bridesmaid's dress. She was smaller all over than Pauline, her cap of dark hair bluntly cut. Perched so far forward as to be practically falling off the bed, she looked like a nervous little bird.

'You'll have to get a move on. The car's waiting outside.'

'But I should be doing something really special.'

'I'll do it.'

'You. You'll make a right mess.'

'Well, just come on then,' said Viv impatiently.

Pauline examined herself in the mirror once more, and set to work.

'Just putting your face on?'

It was Harriet, their mother, checking their progress. Neither of them wanted to look at her, and Pauline just nodded, carrying on with her little brushes. Harriet gently shook out Pauline's veil, and stroked her hair, before she sat down on the bed.

'Well, you both look very nice.'

Pauline stood up. Her eyelids, cheekbones and lips were now more in focus, but the general effect was not much of an improvement. 'I'm frightened,' she whispered. No one responded.

Pauline, Viv and their mother slowly descended the stairs, to the claps of those waiting. The chauffeur, hired to drive the Rolls, and John, the father of the bride, smiled benignly. The two little bridesmaids, Melanie and Sarah, their minds befuddled with fairy tales and soap operas, gaped at a vision of glamour. Their wedding, it was, and no one could take it away from them. Their chance to dress up and be noticed.

Father and daughter got into the Rolls. Pauline had never

2

been in one before, and she felt it might be her only chance. She fingered the leather, shivering at its softness. John turned to her and smiled, taking her fingers from the seat and squeezing them. Pauline leant back: too soon, the journey would be over. Viv, Harriet, and the little bridesmaids got into the car behind – a cheaper one. Viv watched Harriet, inscrutable, placidly staring out of the window.

It was a red-brick church, solid, a respectable working-class building. The bridal party processed rigidly up the aisle, Pauline seeing all the other occasions she had gone up the same aisle as a guide at church parade flash before her eyes. As they did so, Ray and his best man turned round – the usual appreciative, loving look. Ray was considered handsome, was handsome. The same long, lean body-type as John, he also had blond hair, but so light as to be nearly colourless. His face was pointed, his eyes blue, his skin perpetually tanned which must, surely, have come out of a bottle.

He looked steadily at Pauline for a few seconds, and then smiled at her. A smile full of love: perhaps he really cared.

(The actual service, the marriage vows, are imprinted so clearly on my mind. I can remember vividly how I felt kneeling behind them, staring at their backs. For just a few seconds, I wished it was me. I can remember my physical reaction: I was bereft, wanting desperately the love and commitment for myself. But Ray, God no, not him. I distrusted him, despised what he was doing to Pauline. As they spoke, the church became very quiet; every shuffle or sentimental sniff imprinted itself on my brain. A rushed job by the vicar, some whispered hymns by the congregation and it was over. They had been joined; were one.)

The wedding photos were just like anyone else's. In a couple, Pauline is pressed against Ray's chest, smiling out towards us coyly, well-protected. What a history behind each picture. All these happy, blessed, chattering people. The family, dividing and multiplying, each of its existing members smiling serenely at the world.

Harriet stood alone and to one side, except when she was

3

wanted for photos. She had no sisters, brothers or parents alive. Viv approached her out of duty, unsure what to say.

'Pauline looks nice,' said Harriet diffidently.

'Does it remind you . . . ?'

'Of Dad? No, thank God.'

Viv wondered what she could say to that.

But when Harriet was wanted for a photo, she and John would be ready once more to play the part of a happy couple, the bride's parents. Ray's parents, both of them stereotypically round and jolly, were the other happy couple. One pair stood on each side of Ray and Pauline. Snapped.

The meal was pleasant, copious and unimaginative. The bridal party sat at a head table: Phil, as best man, was expected to chat up Viv.

'Your turn next, eh?'

Phil addressed his first remark to Viv over the chicken. He thought her cold, childish, a burden, but with a possible improvement factor in several years' time.

'So they say. I'm not interested, though.'

'Want to play around, eh? What about trying me?'

Christ, he thought. I'm only joking. She looked as though she wanted to throw up.

'No, thanks.' God, what a prospect. 'Anyway, I'm only sixteen.'

'Hey, Phil!'

Ray shouted – he was four people away.

'Listen to what my wife just said.' He spoke the words familiarly, possessively. 'Go on, Pauline, tell him.'

She looked down at the remains on her plate. Eventually, she said: 'I wanted to know what the Parson's Nose was.'

Phil guffawed; Pauline giggled shyly.

'Aren't you stupid, eh?' said Ray affectionately, putting his arm around her, squeezing her.

'Tell her, did you?'

'Yeah, yeah, he told me.'

Viv didn't laugh along with the others; she looked at Pauline with distaste. 'I bet you know, eh?' said the voice in her ear.

4

Phil dug Viv in the ribs, feeling her skinny against the bodice of her bridesmaid's dress.

'Yes, I know.' She looked him up and down, defying further response.

He made a speech, of course, full of the typical jokes about wedding nights, although everyone knew the pair had been having it off for years. John made a speech, too, and read the telegrams. They weren't very funny.

Then the disco, started by the anniversary waltz incompetently shuffled by Pauline and Ray, Pauline holding her dress up in her right hand.

'Come on, time for us to have a go.'

Phil trailed Viv around the floor, together with a few other couples. She didn't like it: it was uncomfortable, and his arms around her were intrusive.

'Not at all like Pauline, are you?'

'Not really.'

At the end of the record, he bowed and walked off. As the circles of dancing people began, Viv joined her parents at the side of the hall and drank. It was the first time that adults had bought her drinks, and she gratefully accepted them. Harriet and John sat together, but they may as well have not: Harriet staring at her drink and the spectacle laid out across the church hall; John chatting to anyone else in earshot. Viv talked to uncles, aunts and people she didn't know, but not to her parents.

'Help me get changed?' Pauline asked Viv eventually. Ray, Phil and some other blokes were downing pint after pint at the other side of the hall.

'We've got to go soon, or Ray'll be too drunk to drive. He says he's exhausted, worn out by his stag night.'

She was very flushed with drink.

'Helen says our reception was much nicer than hers.'

'Well, you spent so much money on it, didn't you?'

Pauline spoke too quickly, excitedly. They went to get her going-away outfit, a blue and white suit and a blue hat.

'I've never seen you in a hat before.'

'Well, I want to do things properly.'

But once outside, when the oohs and aahs and kisses were

over, someone took her hat, and it was soon thrown about the churchyard, people clambering over the graves to get it.

Traditionally, the car had been covered in shaving foam and given a tail of tin cans. Ray feigned surprise, and drove off shakily. Putting her hand on the arm of the person next to her to steady herself, Viv was surprised to find it was Phil. She withdrew it as though his arm would burn her.

'Oh, come on,' he said wearily. 'Let's have another dance.'

Too tired to complain, they went back to dance. As soon as she could, Viv returned to her drunken relatives. Quickly, as quickly as possible, they took her home.

I remember lying in bed that night, automatically listening for the answering breathing in the next bed, and feeling surprised when it wasn't there.

And now, now I look back into the past to try to find out what went wrong. Sitting here in my room, so far in many ways from the wedding. I can still see it in the mirror. My life, Pauline's life, Ray's and everybody else's played out again and again. What have we done?

Is there an answer?

THE PRESENT

What is it, what? I wake up and it's quite dark, the tendrils of the trees coming in where I haven't put up any curtains.

Now I remember, it's coming back to me slowly, discreetly. I did it. Or, to put it more clearly, it happened because of me. It was something I had wanted to do for such a long time, the culmination of many nights of plotting, planning and hatred. And no one would ever, could ever suspect, because I had no motive, no means, no whatever else they say you have to have in detective stories and on the TV. They never stop to consider the power of the mind. God, it was fun, enjoyable, and anyway it served him right.

I laughed and then, liking the sound, I did it again. I hoped that Eric and Sheila didn't hear, but if they did they probably thought I was talking in my sleep. It was something existing outside myself, proving that I existed, too.

The right word to describe this state of mind is glee.

I was light with exhaustion, each limb sinking into the softness of the bed, wrapped around with the duvet. Knowing that I could stay there, that I had the luxury of falling back to sleep whenever I felt like it. Terrific.

Drifting off, I felt myself smaller and smaller in the bed, sinking into the floor as the ceiling withdrew into the distance. But that was all right, too.

Viv's life had carried on in fundamentally the same fashion for a year. Every day in the week she got out of bed at seven forty-five, so that she could catch the train, and then the tube, to her office just off Tottenham Court Road. Viv saw herself as a Londoner. Born and bred in the suburbs, living

7

in the suburbs still – although a different one – she actually enjoyed the travelling, looking at the commuters, wondering about their lives.

For this year, she had worked as a secretary for *Women's Day* magazine, a down-market, very slightly glossy monthly. Her colleagues: Jean, her boss, chief sub-editor. She was efficient, spoke rarely. Hair piled on top of her head, glasses at the end of her nose, she looked like a early Sixties cartoon as she worked steadily at her desk. Carly, half-American, wore a fur coat whenever she got half the chance. Despite her affluent, gushing manner, she was friendly and critically honest about herself. Debbie, Carly's fellow sub, was slightly older than Viv, and lived with a man in Primrose Hill. Her long hair and flowery dressing bringing to mind a Laura Ashley-variety country girl, she was mild and quiet.

Viv's job was quite straightforward: first thing, to take all the people in her section coffee. (Thereafter, they all took turns.) Typing. Everyone typed, but she had to type things ready for the printers. How interesting this was depended on what she had to type. Financial and legal things, boring. There was little telephone answering, because the public didn't know their number. Nor were there letters to write from dictation. But she had to run many messages, taking photocopies, and looking up back numbers of the magazine in the library.

At lunchtime, she could look round the shops, sit in Soho Square if it was warm enough, go and watch the buskers in Covent Garden, have lunch with people from the office or friends who happened to find themselves in the area. Often, Viv just sat at her desk with sandwiches and a book.

Around five, five thirty, Viv caught tube and train in the oppostie direction. Then, there were several possibilities awaiting her. Cooking or not cooking, depending on whether it was her turn. Going to the pub, where a lot of men she knew slightly would talk about politics and try to confide their troubles to her, and women she knew slightly would talk about what they were doing, which included politics, and would try to involve her, thinking that, despite her apparent interest, it was impossible ever to get close to her, to see what she really thought. She was too elusive.

Then some days she and Eric, one flat-mate, would go and see a band in a pub. Or she would go with the other flat-mate Sheila, to the cinema or local theatre. Their house in Lewisham was known as a focus for Labour Party activists – but she didn't belong. Quite often the house hosted Labour Party socials, and after-meeting gatherings, and desperate discussions which she would leave and go to bed. To Viv, it all seemed a front of activity which contrasted with her inactive life. She was both within their world and without it.

I can remember the day's events clearly. In the morning, I spilt a cup of coffee and slightly burnt my hand. It didn't affect my typing. Carly bought three bunches of daffodils, which she arranged artistically in two small vases in the office, incorporating delicate pieces of fern.

On the tube to Charing Cross, there were two drunk blokes. They had suits on, two office types. They reeled onto the packed tube, swayed as it began to move off, threatening to land on those sitting down.

'Here, John,' said the smaller one. 'What do these remind you of?'

The second one was sharply angled and spotty. He guffawed: 'Cocks.'

I was sure they were putting on their working-class accents. It irritated me even more. The quality of their suits made me think they were pretty posh.

'Yeah,' the first one continued. 'It's that bit on the end, innit, and the way they dangle.'

This provoked giggles from the audience, eyes turned to laps, and looks of outrage. But they were encouraged by any response.

'What d'you reckon, love?' they said to the woman next to me. She looked embarrassed. They laughed, and swaggered off the tube at Charing Cross.

What really motivated people like that, I wondered on the train. Would they wake up tomorrow and despise themselves, or think it was a great joke? They seemed so far removed from me that I found it hard to believe they existed at all. Like Ray: a vicious creep if ever there was one. Visions of him floated across the south-east London landscape, reflected in the dirty train windows. Ray laughing: at me, at Pauline, at some offensive joke he'd just told. Ray shouting: at nothing, when he was drunk; at Pauline, because she'd put something away and he couldn't find it. Ray eating like a pig every time I went round there for tea (and still thin as a rake).

Where was his human feeling? I mean, presumably he had some, or Pauline wouldn't have wanted to go out with him.

But it was this which made me think, well, if he's not even human . . . And every time I looked at him all I saw was a collection of cardboardy bits, each tenuously held to the other by string . . .

The woman sitting next to me: she was a person, flesh and blood. She read her hefty paperback, and from time to time she ran her hand up and down her tights to check no hairs had grown back. She passed the test.

And the tired-looking man, middle-aged, whose specks of dandruff nearly reached his gold-rimmed glasses. I could imagine him with his secretary, trying to boss her about, but she seeing through it and treating him with contempt. He passed the test. Just.

Ray didn't; he was just an undeserving collection of odds and ends.

It was growing quite chilly as I got out at the station.

Viv was lying flat on her stomach, hands by her sides, head

10

turned so she could stare out of the window. It was eight thirty, and pretty well dark, but the light from the street turned the room grey-orange. Viv had been lying there since she came home from work, her shoes still on, her black trousers with the creases of wear, her jumper keeping her warm because the house was always draughty even with the electric fire. She looked very young in that position: her short, dark hair covered most of her face, although you could just see the curve of her cheek. She was also rather small, with the dimensions of a mature twelve- or thirteen-year-old.

She luxuriated in her comfort and allowed herself to wonder from time to time whether Eric had got the dinner ready yet. He was pretty damn late tonight. The usual time was nearer seven. She could hear Sheila shuffling about in her own room, and wondered what she was doing. Probably both Sheila and Eric thought she was asleep. She smiled.

'Viv – it's your mum on the phone.'

She sighed. It had been so comfortable there, and now this. Viv sat on the edge of the bed, and fiddled with the buckles on her shoes.

'Viv – come on.'

Eric sounded irritable. Perhaps he'd been caught in the middle of some tricky bit of cooking. Viv shut the door and began to go slowly downstairs.

The contact between Viv and Harriet, her mother, was spasmodic. Since Harriet had persisted in moving to Wiltshire and setting up house with another woman, her family had treated her as selfish and slightly crazy. Her contact with her younger daughter was generally confined to the occasional letter. Phone calls were pretty out of the ordinary.

'Hello, Mum, how are you?'

'It's Ray,' she said abruptly. 'He's dead.'

Viv could find nothing to say.

11

Harriet had often found herself irritated by Viv's lack of reaction. Pauline had always been different, had showed what she felt, but anything could be going on inside Viv's head. She could only be sure of Viv's reactions when she had done something which Viv found ridiculous. Then Viv would sigh, raise her eyes to heaven, and say something like 'really'.

When Harriet told her that Ray had been found dead, she didn't react as Harriet would have expected. She said 'oh', and then 'oh dear'. She didn't ask why, or from what, or when, just 'oh'. But she had plenty of concern about Pauline.

'Pauline's disappeared,' Harriet said.

'No.'

She sounded aghast, terrified.

'How do you know?'

'The police contacted me, of course.'

Surprise came to Harriet over the phone, as though Viv had forgotten the police existed.

'And what are they doing about it?' A cold tone.

'Looking for her.'

Harriet was annoyed by her distance, denseness.

'I'll be going round there tomorrow.'

'Can I come?'

'If you like.'

Harriet was puzzled yet again. Viv: her reactions were none of the common sort. She didn't even want to know how her mother had a key.

Viv dashed upstairs, past the kitchen door, full of the questions which she had not dared to ask her mother. Pauline. She threw herself back on the bed, stunned sick. What had happened to her? Did they think she was dead, too? She suddenly realised that she had not asked her mother any questions about Ray's death.

In her mind's eye, she could see him, an unerasable picture. He was propped up in a chair, in the corner of that modern bedroom of theirs, curtains open onto the street. And there was blood everywhere, on the carpet, red mixed with pink, a few specks on the wall, dried already on the observer's hands, face and clothes and, especially, on Ray. His eyes stared, dense and blue, growing deeper by the second. He was rigid – you could push him with one finger and he would topple over. There: now he was on the floor, his body still curved, his knees to his chest. Quite dead.

'Dinner.'

The voice was becoming increasingly urgent. It ignored the fact that Viv had more important things to do than heed it. It came upstairs, closer to her all the time, and finally spoke outside the door.

'Viv – are you asleep?'

'Oh. What? No. Coming.'

Her voice sounded hesitant, anxious, but she dragged her body up, slowly, heavily, off the bed, and switched the light on. Things seemed so much more normal with the light on. But Pauline, what about Pauline?

Eric was already dishing out the lentil stew when Viv got downstairs. He looked up at her accusingly.

'Sorry,' she said. 'I was miles away.'

He piled a yellow heap onto her plate, and indicated the rice.

'Oh, it doesn't matter.' He paused. 'This thing took a hell of a long time cooking.'

'It's nice,' said Sheila encouragingly.

'Great.' Viv nodded her head.

'Oh, that's good.' Eric begrudged them this. The day had not gone well. He felt – although he wouldn't have described it as such – sulky.

'Did your mum have anything interesting to say?' asked Sheila.

'Do they ever?' Viv replied.

'Well, she doesn't ring very often.'

'True. But it still wasn't very interesting.'

'I quite like my parents, in fact,' said Eric, swirling his dinner in circles. He felt bloody-minded.

13

'Liking doesn't have anything to do with it,' continued Viv. 'I just don't understand my parents at all and they don't understand me.'

A tetchy silence took over. Sheila felt compelled to bring the other two together. Her tolerance for sulking was minimal although she did resent being forced into the role of peace-maker.

'Anyone coming out for a drink later?' she asked.

'Maybe,' said Eric. He usually did.

'No,' said Viv.

'Oh, come on,' Sheila said. 'You never seem to go out any more, you're just shut in your room all the time.'

'I'm having a nervous breakdown,' said Viv stoically.

'No, you're not. I want you to come out for a drink with me tonight,' said Sheila.

'OK.' Viv didn't care one way or the other. She liked Sheila and it would make her happy.

The three of them seemed to be giving sexual relationships a wide berth for the present, each for different reasons, and therefore spent a good deal of time with their flat-mates. As far as Viv was concerned, she had simply lost the inclination, and had not slept with anyone for the past three years. This celibacy had not lessened her desire to have a wonderful passionate relationship with someone, sometime. Not now. Sex was something other people did, and she had been another person the last time she had done it.

That was how Viv saw herself: unconnected. Still, there were people who would have liked to be connected with her. Principal among them was Eric, who was just waiting for his moment to pounce. Figuratively, of course: he prided himself on being non-sexist. He saw Viv as soft, lonely: how he feared he might be, too.

Walking to the pub, Viv was conscious of herself bobbing

14

up and down beside Eric. He was a very tall man, and she a short woman, and the contrast was ridiculous. Sheila, on the other side of Eric, was of medium height, a portly woman with golden-black skin. She was saying something or other to Eric; Viv was not paying attention although she did want her mind taken off things.

Pushing open the pub door, Viv was conscious of putting on another face. There were people she recognised sitting at a table in the centre of the room.

'Thanks, Eric, I'll have half of lager.'

They carried their drinks over to the table.

'So, thought you'd never come!'

Josh was speaking, a small man with spiky red hair. The other two at the table were Linda, a female version of Josh with lots of make-up, and Jackie, a good friend of Sheila's, a small, very dark black woman with short hair and huge earrings. Eric and Sheila clustered around her, and Viv pulled up a seat next to Josh as Linda went to the loo.

'How are you then?' Viv asked.

'Oh, you know,' he shrugged. 'My relationship with Linda has broken up.'

'Ah,' said Viv, and thought: I don't want to know.

'We were meeting tonight to talk about it, but there's no point, really. She says I'm too clinging,' he concluded sadly, staring wistfully into his beer. They remained silent, counting the seconds until Linda returned.

'Perhaps I could come and cry on your shoulder sometime. I feel so awful, and you're so . . . such a . . . so sympathetic.'

'Sure, whenever.'

They had both spotted Linda coming, both felt the embarrassment that she must feel, knowing they were talking about her.

'How's things?' said Viv woodenly.

'So-so. How about you?'

'Oh, the same. Life plods along.'

'Dear, dear,' said Linda. 'This maudlin attitude isn't like you.'

'Oh, things aren't that bad. But I'm allowed to get depressed sometimes, aren't I?'

A burst of laughter from Sheila, Eric and Jackie.

'Yes, I think we'll allow you that,' Linda said. 'Nothing specific, though?'

'No,' said Viv thoughtfully. 'Nothing specific.'

Linda gazed at Viv intently, while Josh continued to stare balefully into his beer.

'That's good.'

At another burst of laughter, they turned their chairs towards the other group. Why couldn't she tell them? What was she afraid of? Oh, she knew the answer only too well: they would use the information against her. It would contaminate her. Besides, how could she explain the things she knew? They would think her unhinged.

'Well, why don't you then?'

Viv looked up suddenly, and all the others laughed.

'Sorry,' she said to Jackie. All the faces peered down at her. She had been staring at the tiny white bubbles patterning her drink.

'We were wondering what it would take to make you join the Labour Party Young Socialists. After all, you're the only one in your household who doesn't belong.'

'Aren't I too old?' said Viv feebly.

'Hardly. Twenty-one's pretty young, in fact.'

'Oh, I'll think about it.'

Jackie was silent. They were all silent. Their faces were crowding in once more. Then someone said something Viv couldn't catch and it was time to go home.

Viv was late. Did Viv honestly think Harriet enjoyed sitting around in a house where someone had just violently died. Where there's still blood on the carpet? That girl has no consideration for others, she thought, particularly Harriet herself, but all others really. After all, who had just come from the country all the way on the M4 and the South

Circular in a traffic jam? God, Harriet thought, how I hate London.

Pauline and Ray bought their house when they got married. Harriet had never liked it, although she hid her feelings at the time, because they felt so proud of it: a house of their own and so young. Ray's parents put down the deposit. It seemed to Harriet a soulless house, in an estate with row upon row of similar soulless houses. A tree here, a privet hedge there, and a few bright front doors. Otherwise nothing.

Harriet watched Viv coming down the road, watched her amble round the corner without looking up at the house. She opened the door as Viv came up the path and bounded towards her, grabbing her round the neck. Viv's body shuddered with sobs as she nuzzled against her shoulder, like a baby.

'Pauline didn't do it,' she said.

'But nobody thinks she did.' said Harriet quizzically. 'You don't even know how he died yet.'

'Oh,' said Viv. 'No. I suppose not.'

Viv's eyes travelled around the hall, into each doorway, as Harriet propelled her into the front room.

'He died in the bedroom, if that's what you're wondering.'

'Oh.'

Again, that bloody non-commital 'oh'.

'I must see it,' she continued.

By the time Harriet had said she wouldn't, Viv was halfway up the stairs. She bounded, two at a time, round the bend, and threw open the door to their room. Then she stopped, positioned against the doorframe, and stared in the direction of the blood. It was flecked everywhere, and, at the bottom of the chair by the window, it was coagulating in a pool. Viv carried on looking and looking, not moving an inch until suddenly she walked rapidly over to the chair and stared with deep concentration at the bloodstain, as though her face was reflected in it.

Then she turned towards Harriet, her expression blank, robbed of her pupils. She took a few steps, heavily, the fourth bringing her straight into Harriet as though she didn't exist.

17

But the shock of that confrontation aroused her, and she twisted her head, and pressed into her mother's neck. Harriet's arms felt bloodless and useless to her, could not express any of what she felt. But they went up stiffly at the elbows and around her.

They sat downstairs, quietly, in the front room full of intricate ornaments.

'Ray was a dreadful man,' Harriet said eventually. Viv sighed.

'Yes, he was.'

They sat for a few moments more.

Then Harriet stood up, brushing off her trousers where a few hairs glistened, and went into the kitchen. The room was bright and clean; spotless, even. Harriet and Viv both felt the contrast with themselves. The tea things, matching the kitchen decor, were easy to hand, and Harriet lay them out on the tray. Walking into the other room, she could hear Viv tut, and swallowed her own annoyance. This over-whelming cuteness was, after all, Pauline's desire, not her own. But giving people the benefit of the doubt had never been one of Viv's strong points.

'There'll be a post-mortem. We'll know about that soon. And then an inquest. Will you be coming?'

'No.'

'You may have to, you know.'

Viv stayed silent, looking at her canvas shoes.

'Don't you want to know what happened? Aren't you going to do anything, apart from sitting there acting peculiar? This is my problem too, you know, my worry too, not just yours.'

Harriet swallowed her regret at this outburst. Viv still looked at her feet, but her face contorted for a few seconds, and she mumbled:

'I'm sorry.'

'Well, look,' Harriet said in a business-like fashion, 'let's try to think logically about Pauline and anywhere she could be.'

Viv's eyes burnt into Harriet as though she could kill her.

18

It was strange to look at the house where I had been such an ordinary and often unwelcome visitor over the past few years and think: that's it. The angles of the building were just the same, the path was the same, everything was the same, and yet it was all totally different. No, I would do it, I would go in. I would do something difficult for a change.

The little path came up to get me, the well-kept roses put out their thorns, and I began to stagger. Something was getting me, bearing down on me; it was retreating, coming forward and retreating again. Then I noticed her face at the window: Mum. She opened the door, watching me lurch up the path, saying nothing. Her eyes summed me up disparagingly, but there was something more behind her gaze. She leaped on me, drawing me into her neck, squashing my nose. It didn't last long.

'How,' I heard her say. 'How?'

I wasn't even certain what she was asking me, but words of defence spilled out of my mouth just the same.

I looked around the hall, and then the whole of downstairs. She said something to me, talked more and more, but I couldn't make out what she was saying. Instead, I went upstairs to see it. There.

And the room was exactly as I had pictured it.

It was deep, the pool of blood. Deep, dark red and begining to smell. Nobody had bothered to clear it up. Perhaps that was something I could do. I must get a cloth, a bucket, some disinfectant. I turned, walking, and there she was. Mum: warm, roundish, a smell that I remembered from years ago. She moved her arms like lumps of wood, but still they were there. I knew that I had felt this comfort before, recognised it from somewhere, but I couldn't remember when. It was intense – claustrophobic and vulnerable together. I couldn't stand it: I moved towards the stairs.

It was a hateful house; I knew that as we sat downstairs saying nothing. It seemed possessed by each hideous little china ornament. I hated Pauline for living there, for furnishing it, for marrying Ray. Ray I hated for himself.

Not that anything could have redeemed it: not my posters, my stuff, myself. It would still have been the same.

'Anything might be happening to her right now,' I remember saying. I don't remember if there was any reply, but I do remember us searching through address books, drawers, making a mess of Pauline's pristine house. There was nothing there of any consequence. To us.

Eventually, I cried. More and more I cried.

Did my brother-in-law really warrant so many tears?

Harriet and Marjorie lived in a cottage. Not a cottage of the picture-book variety, but a cottage simply in that it seemed too small to be called a house. Built between the wars, the rooms were cramped and odd: cold in winter and almost fetid in summer. But they felt it homely, and were happy there, happier than they had been with their husbands.

They had met at an evening class: 'Fresh Start for Women'. Ten middle-aged women, mostly divorced or separated, met and discussed their lives, looked at what they could and couldn't do. Some women moved off into computers and word processing. Marjorie and Harriet got together and, with their alimony, had lived for five years in the country. Once a week they each had a day waitressing, Majorie occasionally made things to sell, but otherwise they depended upon the munificence of their ex-husbands.

Marjorie was prepared for an evening walk with coat and wellingtons when Harriet got back. A robust, attractive woman with shoulder-length, streaked blonde hair, she always seemed the picture of health beside Harriet. She looked like a country hippy, rather than someone who has seen too much of life.

'Hello.'

They embraced, rather uncertainly, and Marjorie drew back to look at Harriet.

'I thought perhaps you'd be staying in town.'

'I don't think Viv would want me to stay with her. I had to come back.'

'Sit down and tell me what's happened.'

'No, Marjorie, later. You go and walk. I'll be here when you get back.'

'Well, can I get you anything?'

'No, no,' said Harriet, shooing her out of the door.

Marjorie did a great many things Harriet found stupid, such as wandering around all night looking at the stars. But her eccentricity was comforting, familiar. Once she had gone out, Harriet roamed around the house, knocking back the whisky. Of course, she had always known that their marriage would come to no good, but not in this way. Thoughts of it went round and round her head: how did he die?

Harriet sat on the edge of the bed, holding the bottle of whisky, and fell backwards. There were many things she could imagine, things that she would not reveal to Viv or Marjorie. Pauline could be dead, he could easily have killed her. Alternatively, she could have killed him. The police would not put her out of her misery, prevaricating, only saying that they were looking for her.

She had got up at six this morning, and now it was nearly eleven. Still her mind would not shut down, and although she had drunk much tea and whisky, she had eaten little. Harriet looked at herself in the mirror: she was wearing all black as usual, rather tatty black, but still the effect was rather dramatic. She put her fingers in her hair and splayed it outwards. It was red – thick and beautiful – full of lights as she let it fall. She was as she wanted to be. So how dare they disturb her life?

Later, she heard Marjorie come back into the house. She heard her feet run up the stairs and go into her room, her faint humming. Help me, she thought, help me. But she didn't go and ask, allowed Marjorie to think her asleep. Somewhere there was a chilling feeling that Marjorie ought to have known, ought to have come in of her own accord, ought not to have been singing, however dirge-like and gentle.

Alone. She was alone with her feelings, and she turned to the softness of her bed for help.

John felt everything was right with his marriage to Penny. She was fifteen years younger than John – his second marriage, but not the second woman with whom he had lived. There had been four of those altogether. But Penny was irresistible: glamorous, alive, interested and interesting. And what she really wanted was him.

They were in bed together: marital, lawful, connubial bliss.

'Time to wake up, darling.'

'What makes you think I'm asleep?'

She leaned over him, and kissed his cheek. They did not make love: there was no need, they could do it in the evening. Still, he felt so tender that he got out of bed, pulled on his neat dressing-gown, and made the coffee. He had recently come into more money: promotion, the sale of his dead mother's semi, meant he could more ably support Penny. She contributed fairly handsomely to the budget, too. It was only that Harriet was still a drain on his income, and probably would always be so, that prevented their living in high style.

'Oh, lovely.'

Their bedroom was light, with a beige shag-pile carpet and fitted furniture. The bed was part of a unit comprising a white wardrobe, half on each side, two bedside tables, and a mirror behind the bed. Penny hauled herself up in bed, adjusted her pretty cotton nightie, drew a hand back through her hair, and smiled.

22

'Put the coffee down a minute, and I'll go and get the papers. I can hear the letterbox.'

She ran lightly down and up the stairs, flinging the papers onto the bed, and quickly got back in. John grabbed the *Express*, she the local. He could feel immediately that something was wrong.

'What is it?'

She passed the paper to him. On the front was a brief description of Ray's death, and the fact that his wife was missing. His eyes stayed on the page, unflinching. But Penny could sense his body growing stiffer, stiffer, stiffer.

'How could they?' he heaved.

She touched his arm through his pyjamas. Silent for a few seconds, John brusquely wrapped himself in his dressing-gown again, and thumped down the stairs. The phone was right at the bottom, and Penny sat at the top, watching him. He was pacing in wide semi-circles around the phone.

'Harriet there . . .'

A pause from his end as he listened to Marjorie. He wasn't exactly becoming less angry, but his sense of desolation was beginning to match his fury, dragging the blood from his face.

'But why the hell didn't anyone think to tell me?'

A few more moments of grunting, and then he muttered: 'Goodbye.'

He walked slowly up the stairs, and sat down next to Penny, quiet, burying his head in her lap.

'They didn't even think to tell me; they didn't even think of it.'

She stroked his head, pressed it into her stomach, caressing him over and over again. She, too, was outraged that they had not considered him, and would have pitied him, had that been allowed.

'Did she tell you what happened?'

'It was only Marjorie. She doesn't know much.'

'Does your dear ex-wife?'

'Don't know.' His voice shook. 'There's a post-mortem. Maybe she's at that.'

'What are you going to do?'

23

'I'll think of something.'

He wasn't very convincing. How could something so appalling be allowed to happen? Besides, to mitigate his general arrogance, he truly loved his daughters. How could they be harmed?

Two days after Ray's death: could that be all?

It was about ten, and they had all had quite a bit to drink. The remains of their curry lay around them as they lolled on the table. Their glasses were still full and the debris of cigarette papers and tobacco were next to Linda. She rolled a deft joint.

Viv's household often had people round for meals, it was easy to cook a bit more and then they could all spend the evening slumping farther and farther over the big kitchen table. Eric, particularly, seemed to enjoy extending hospitality. At present he and Alfie, Jackie's brother, were pontificating about black sections in the Labour Party.

'Of course,' Eric said, 'you'll have to fight tooth and nail to get anything out of them. They know where the power lies and they're damn well going to keep it there.'

'We're used to it,' said Alfie.

'It's so entrenched, that type of institutionalised, we-know-what's-best-for-you racism.'

Around the table, there seemed to be a conspiracy. Eric, and to some extent Alfie, went on and on; the women smirked at each other.

'Oh, yes, and who exactly are you talking about?' said Jackie, amused, her head slightly on one side.

'Well, the old guard, you know.'

'That's right,' said Alfie dreamily.

'In so far as he goes, Eric's always right,' Sheila muttered.

'What was that?' he said.

'I said you were always right.'

He looked slightly aggressive, and Sheila sighed loudly. 'You *are* always right.'

Eric felt that somehow he was being laughed at, so he swallowed a gulp of his cider. Viv wondered for the hundredth time what people talked about.

'We're all talking a load of crap,' she said.

'I thought we were talking about fucking politics,' Alfie said.

'Maybe we are, maybe we aren't,' said Jackie. Sheila said nothing. She looked at Jackie as though she was trying to remember every detail, and suddenly she left the room. Soon, erotic saxophone sounds were coming through loudly on the extension speakers. Sheila resumed her position next to Jackie.

'Whose record is this?' Linda's voice suddenly reminded everyone of her existence: this was unusual – Linda didn't often allow you to forget her.

'Yours?' she continued, looking at Viv.

'Sure is.'

Viv looked at her carefully, then back at the others. Her body, her mind, was possessed with longing, free-floating, unattached, victimless. Overcome with dope-induced desire, she sat arms wrapped around her knees, staring at her black trousers. They were all silent.

'Let's have a truth session,' Viv said eventually.

'A what?'

'A truth session. For instance, I ask Linda who she'd go to bed with in this room if someone held a gun to her head. Or I'd ask someone else who was their worst enemy.'

'Sounds ridiculous,' said Eric.

They stayed quiet, involved in the music. But Viv wanted to be far from it, as far as possible. She looked at their groupings: Eric and Alfie, facing each other. Alfie near his sister, who was almost squashed against Sheila. Only Linda seemed alone, tearing a tissue into small pieces and dropping them from a height into the ashtray. Who was she, Viv wondered?

She stood up, gripped the table firmly, and said: 'I'm going to bed.' She opened her mouth again, and then said: 'No addendums.'

'Addenda.'

'Smart alec.' Viv couldn't even remember who had said it. Out the door, up the stairs, onto the bed, lie down.

Pretence. I had not really inhaled much of that dope. I liked the sensation of sucking it, of feeling the smoke come in, but then I always got rid of it, spat it out quite conscientiously.

Or was I fooling myself a little bit? I lay back on my bed, staring at the ceiling, falling. I wanted to fall into a bed, another bed, but not alone. Downstairs, they were a long, long way away.

The dream was real, vivid – in Yugoslavia, where I had been on holiday a couple of years ago, but a dream Yugoslavia. I was walking to the grocers, through the mountains, climbing higher and higher, invigorated, exhilarated. Achievement step by step.

But before I had a chance to reach the grocers, I was ambushed. Khaki-covered men, waving sub-machine guns, leaped from behind trees which had suddenly sprung up and levelled the guns at me. Then as I, stuck, tried to relay messages between my brain and feet, Ray swung down, like an orang-utan, from one of the trees. He laughed wholeheartedly, like he'd discovered a good joke. Grabbing a gun from one of his henchmen, he pressed it against my throat and said calmly: 'The man who had power over women.'

Then he began tenderly to caress my body with it, smiling indulgently at my legs, which were shaking so much that I was sinking to the ground.

'Don't worry, it won't go off,' he said.

He was sure that was all my fear, but then I began to feel the gun taking my skin off in its path around my body.

Suddenly my eyes were open, but I could still feel the gun's path. The fear was still there. Of course. But was he? I looked around, eyelids anxiously flickering.

I felt slightly queasy as I got up. My head span – down to the kitchen to get some milk and aspirin. The clock radio glowed two thirty-two, and I felt slightly worried about getting up for work in the morning. Dirty, unclean, to do this to myself.

The light was still on in the kitchen, strange so late, the quiet so deafening. I tiptoed down the stairs, hand for comfort on the banister. Soon I could see them, still sitting on separate chairs, arms around each other, kissing, tentatively but with passion. They they let go of each other but kept close, foreheads together. Sheila and Jackie. My friends.

The knot in my stomach was pressing back, back, back. My hand, heavy and sweaty, clutching the banister. Oh, well. I turned and went upstairs again. I took most of my clothes off and got back into bed. I could feel tears growing up in my eyes, and trickling backwards to my pillow. Oh, well. Maybe I would have love some time or another.

Harriet had spent the day waitressing in the tea shop – her one-day-a-week job, which would bring in about twenty pounds if the customers were reasonable. She was one of two women there, and took over on the usual woman's day off.

This was not a good day. People came and went, asked for toast, cakes, set lunch; laughed or stared into space or were tight-lipped. Harriet could hardly stand it. The weight pushing her shoulder blades down into her back: it was purgatory.

'Can you tell me anything, anything at all?'

'Perhaps you could ring back later, madam. We've spoken to her husband's parents already.'

Several times, Harriet rang the police. Always the same

reply. Evasive. Later; ring back; we don't know. She could hardly move, take the orders, assemble the trays, put the dirty dishes in the sink.

When she got home, the police station was engaged. Marjorie was muddy, healthy from digging in the garden. She came to embrace Harriet.

'You look terrible,' she said.

'Yes.'

'And?'

'And nothing. I keep trying to find out and no one wants to tell me anything.'

'Try again while I get you some tea and a hot-water bottle.'

Harriet kept her head in her hands for a few minutes and gathered her wits. The phone to the police station rang blankly once, twice, three times.

'It's Mrs Foster,' she said. 'About the Armstrong case. My son-in-law, daughter.'

'Ah, yes.' She was passed over.

'Now then.' The senior policeman paused, shuffled a few pieces of paper.

'You realise that this is only the post-mortem, not the inquest. That will come later.'

Harriet, her mind in suspension, grunted.

'Well, it would appear, judging from the angle, strength and number of the wounds, that it could be murder or self-inflicted. There are, naturally, several complicating factors. For instance, no fingerprints were found on the handle of the weapon. Then, of course, there is the matter of your daughter's disappearance. It would, we feel, be unwise to speculate as to why. The main thing is to find her. Are you following me, Mrs Foster?'

'What are you trying to say?'

'Briefly, Mrs Foster, that she could have been murdered, that she could have murdered him, that she has run off with someone else.'

Harriet sniffed. 'Oh.'

'We are, of course, investigating, making a most thorough search for her. So I would ask you once again, Mrs Foster, if there is anything you can tell us, no matter how insignificant.'

'If I could, I'd have told you already. We've already discussed their marital relationship.'

'Well, maybe something will come to mind.'

'If it does, I'll tell you at once.'

'You do that, Mrs Foster.'

Harriet headed straight for the Scotch.

'Oh dear.' Marjorie picked up the bottle, and held it from her, as Harriet downed the measure in her glass.

'Bad?'

'It could be anything. Pauline might have done it, or he might have killed her and he could have killed himself.'

'Great.'

Marjorie wrapped a blanket around Harriet, and gave her the hot-water bottle. It was quite cold in the cottage, but not that cold. She placed the tea in Harriet's hand and took away the whisky.

'Drink that instead.'

Harriet cupped her hands around the tea, and sipped it slowly, in the manner of an invalid. Marjorie studied her carefully.

'So what can you do now?'

Harriet shrugged.

'Ring his parents, perhaps. But I don't want to. Anyway, I don't know their number.'

'Never heard of directory enquiries?'

Harriet stared into her cup, miserably, looking for patterns, for guidance in it.

'I'll ring them.'

Marjorie squeezed Harriet's arm, feeling it firm and fleshy under her fingers.

'Now.'

Harriet got up, dragged herself from her chair, scarcely feeling her aching feet. To the phone, the operator, the number.

'It's ringing.'

It rang and rang and rang.

'There's no answer. There's no bloody answer.'

Harriet slammed the phone down, and wept.

For the rest of the evening, she was cosseted. She had

nothing to do but eat and drink from the bottle of whisky she had taken back from Marjorie. Her mind was blank. Marjorie sat knitting, a luxurious wool and silk jumper which she hoped to sell at the craft market.

'Why don't you go to bed?' she said. It was nine thirty.

'Well, I'll have a bath.'

She lay there, soaking. It was fantastic, scarcely believable. She was becoming truly clean, symbolically clean, washing parts of herself away.

Viv's third day at work passed automatically. She functioned, for most of the time, thoughtless, every now and then the sense of calamity hitting her. By the evening, the preceding ten hours had evaporated. A pity, she felt; she wanted to be alive. But by the evening, the necessity to appear normal kept her, afraid, in her room.

'What's with Viv?' Sheila asked Eric as they absent-mindedly washed up the dinner things.

'Who knows? But whatever it is, it's getting worse,' he said. 'She runs away if you try to talk to her, and hardly leaves her room, only comes out when it's unavoidable.'

'She was a bit kind of disjointed last night, didn't you think?'

Eric smiled back at Sheila: 'Well, she's not going to tell me what's wrong, is she?'

'Oh, come on, Eric, she likes you as much as me.'

'I don't think so.'

'She and I aren't nearly as close as we used to be, or hadn't you noticed?'

'I had, but I figured it was all part of the same withdrawal process.'

'Perhaps.'

Sheila was quiet for a few moments, running two fingers back and forth against the table edge.

'But, Sheila,' Eric continued, 'I do think you'd do better than I would talking to her. Women tend to stick together.'

He wiped the table around her fingertips.

'Yes, we do.'

Sheila lit a cigarette and inhaled, blowing the smoke away from Eric's face.

'And speaking of women sticking together, what's going on between you and Jackie, eh?'

He raised one of his eyebrows and wiggled it, a trick when he was trying to be amusing. Sheila laughed: she had been expecting this, had a measured amount of irritation prepared, and her laugh dispersed it.

'What, indeed.'

The phone rang.

'Viv, it's your dad.'

Viv's footsteps steadily tripped downstairs.

'Dad,' she said.

The kitchen door was just ajar, and they could hear her in the hall.

'This is a bit odd,' whispered Sheila. 'Viv's parents don't usually ring up like this.'

'I don't know, Dad', they could hear Viv saying. 'You'll have to ask Mum.'

Sheila and Eric were quiet.

'I don't know whether she's spoken to them or not.'

'No, Dad, no.'

'I'm sorry.'

Viv put the phone back on the hook, and was on the point of going back upstairs when she saw the kitchen door open. They must have been listening. Her face flushed hot and red and she knew she must go in, pretend nothing had happened.

'Hi,' she said languidly. 'Got a ciggie? I seem to have run out.'

Eric passed over a packet of tobacco and some papers.

'Are you OK?' he said paternally, his voice low.

She laughed. It was a cold laugh, slightly cracked, but she hoped they wouldn't notice.

'Oh, yes, I'm all right.'

31

She thought they would be chary of asking more, and she was right.

'It's just that you seem a bit depressed,' he continued.

'I am a bit. Not a lot.'

They were ganging up on her, two against one.

'We were worried about you,' Sheila said.

'There's no need,' Viv reassured them.

They were quiet, tense.

'I've got to go out, actually,' Viv said. 'See you later.' She shut the door behind her quietly, and walked straight out.

It was rather a clammy night, not too bad for a walk to an appointment, but Viv had nowhere to go. She just couldn't stand being in, and didn't want anyone's concerned sympathy. Didn't want to think, much less talk. Her father ringing up and wanting news when there wasn't any. Everything seemed to be going wrong. Not disastrously yet, but that could be coming. Pauline, Pauline. Thinking about her brought on the panic, the sickness, weakness, contraction in the chest. She had not bargained for that.

Viv walked along bouncily, quickening into a sort of jog to keep her spirits up. Why had she had that dream last night? It might as well have come out of a psychology textbook on Freud, a subject which she had studied for A-level. Guns, bloody guns. How clichéd can you get?

Round and round and round and when she returned, they were out. Coming home to silence, Viv felt a great sense of anti-climax. Now nothing would happen. She went upstairs to try to make up some of last night's sleep.

Sheila knocked quietly when she came back from the pub, and opened the door when she got no answer. All that was showing above the duvet was Viv's head, a picture of sweetness, innocence and contentment.

*

Once again, wide awake, dark, eyes open, what's going on, what? The fear: of everything and nothing. What was going on in the far, recessed corners of my room, in the parts where I could not see?

The sadness of death, the passing of a good person, the washing over of tremendous pain from head to foot. Where did it come from?

Another dream. I was with Ray in a restaurant, slightly hazy, distant. Pretty soon he left me, wandering away to join a group, leaving me lonely.

Then he came back towards me, hands out, beseeching. His eyes were soft, hurt, pleaded with me.

'Why do you hate me so much, why?' His pain was evident. 'You misconstrue me all the time.'

I said nothing. Perhaps it was true. I got up, trying to get far away, but I could not. His eyes followed me, further and further until I had to wake up.

Was he good?

THE PAST

Not all that long ago, Harriet's main emotion had been disappointment with life. She looked back at the ambitions of her youth and she was bitter. None of it had happened.

This feeling didn't wait to emerge as a mid-life crisis; it started in her twenties, when she was having the girls and when they were toddlers. She would never harm them: they were her children and she loved them. She could not regret their being. Not exactly. But she had not chosen them, they had happened. They were part of adulthood, and while they knew what they expected of her, she did not know what she expected of them. As a mother, she just was. It was not that she did not know what she wanted any more but that, on the surface at least, she had forgotten about it.

Harriet felt as a schoolgirl that there was a great future mapped out for her in some artistic field. She was not sure precisely where: indeed, to try to discover felt too risky, but she was sure it would seek her out and discover her. At school, she was not exactly lonely: she had friends, with whom she would discuss this and that. But there was no intellectual coterie (her school was far too down to earth), and she longed for it as she sat in her bedroom night after night, reading Françoise Sagan, listening to jazz records, and smoking out of an open window the cigarettes her parents would not permit. As she looked around her bedroom with its flowered wallpaper in vertical patterns, and the pastel candlewick bedspread, her excitement at the future knew no bounds.

So she was disappointed, at eighteen, to discover that not only did her parents think it was pointless her trying for university, but that they wanted her to work in a bank. She did. She was compliant, liked people to feel she was doing the right thing, whether she agreed or not. Harriet was surprised, in a way, that her parents did not also think her destined for great things. They could not go on supporting her, they said.

Her attitude towards the bank was in many ways similar to her attitude at school. It had to be tolerated, so it was. Its deficiencies were compensated for in daydreams and, if possible, in actions to improve the situation. With this in mind, every weekend she took the train from the suburbs into London, abandoning the grey tailored suit she wore when she was Miss Evans and instead dressing always in black. She wore straight black trousers, black jumpers, black pumps, and her hair loose – something which the bank would not have allowed. She would sit on the platform for the train in expectation of something happening. Wonderful men (always shadowy) would meet her. Interesting, bohemian women would invite her to share their flats, offer her who knew what (she certainly wasn't sure).

But little happened. Much of the time she would just wander around, go into pubs and coffee bars occasionally, and frequently get importuned by men, but never the ones she wanted. They were often smelly, old, boring or loutish, or simply asked her how much. She didn't fancy that, although she wasn't sure why. She had no moral objections, and, as she didn't really believe in her own fertility, didn't believe she would get pregnant. Still, she backed off.

Not all Harriet's social life was taken up with these solitary meanderings. The young, unmarried people at the bank would go out together, and so Harriet came, eventually, to be going out with John.

John came to work at the bank six months after Harriet. She took little notice of him: he had fair hair, slightly limp, and wore similarly limp suits. He liked banking, he said, because one had power over money and therefore over people. He did not say this to Harriet personally, but to people in general, and when she heard it she knew that he was not for her. Not dramatic enough, not exceptional.

The young people at the bank were in the habit of drinking together at a bar in the local hotel. There were some six of them: two women, four men, or thereabouts. No sexual connotations were overt, although the men discussed the women rather scathingly when they weren't there. Also, there was jocular banter, chattering about how the women might or might not, and when they decided could they please tell them. But no one took it more seriously than that.

John singled Harriet out, began to talk to her when they were drinking. Talk seriously. She would sit and listen, as he told her of his plans to manage a bank eventually. The first time he asked her to go out with him on their own, she said no out of hand. He had been so abashed, so obviously disappointed, that when she saw him next, she was unable to refuse again. He was overjoyed, his face shone and even his clothes perked up a bit. She realised, aghast, that he must be in love with her.

After a few dates, she became more fond of him. He confided in her more and more, and the novelty of being truly loved overwhelmed her. She began to laugh a little more. But she could not tell him what she had planned for herself, that she, too, wanted something although she couldn't yet tell what. Instead, she concentrated on listening, saying what he wanted her to say. And in return they went out to dinner together, and went dancing. They walked around London together.

So they were married. He had proposed and she had accepted. Unsure whether it was what she wanted, although sure enough it would be a change from her present life, she accepted because any sign of doubt brought a dreadful wave of disappointment to John's eyes. She could not bear to disappoint, especially not him, who had been so good to her. And they had not had sex: she had refused when pressed, and he had left off, instead seeing a friend of a friend who would always do it if you asked politely enough. She faced up stoically to the fact that, after marriage, she would have to.

In the wedding photos, the couple looked happy. She smiled for the camera rather uncertainly: so becoming, they thought. They should indeed have been happy, for the wedding cost her parents a lot of money. But this they did not begrudge. It was no more than what one owed a daughter. And so, she was allowed to give up work, which

36

she didn't like, learned that sex was quite tolerable, if one's husband cared, and read poetry quietly, in the daytime, when no one could find her out. Soon, she was pregnant.

Roused from her sleep, her dreams, her peace, by a wail loud, insistent. A snatched nipple comforts this tiny human, so perfect.

Harriet is far from her mother, distant from her husband, and whenever did she have any friends?

Her mind is glazed, can't concentrate, can scarcely remember that the milk bill needs paying, there is a bucket of nappies to be boiled, must buy the carrots. John works late, always, returns to marvel at his little daughter. From afar.

Out pushing the pram, Harriet realises through a thick fog that the day is wonderful, that it is spring and the daffodils are in glorious abundance. In the pram, there is a miracle. It smiles as it wakes, looks at the sky. Her legs give way and, at a park bench, it cries. Get up; go on.

Of course, one gets used to the self-denial, is overwhelmed by the positive.

It's so much easier the second time, so two years later, along came another one.

'Oh, Viv, don't. You really are so silly. Stop it.'

Pauline was busy making a sandcastle. Neatly, orderly, she packed bucket after bucket with sand, upturning each bucket's worth next to another. Now her sister was threatening to wreck it, flicking sand on it. Her anger was rising.

'No. Stop it.'

Viv was peeved. Nothing she could do was right. No one was taking any notice of her.

'Pauline won't let me play.'

Viv tugged at her mother's swimsuit. There was little of it, and her mother only warily opened one eye.

'Why don't you sunbathe then?'

'It's so boring.'

'Stop whining.' Her father, tanned, very lean, looked up from his paper towards his daughters. He did not like playing, something which their mother would do.

'Pauline, give her a go.'

'Why should I?'

'Don't be selfish.'

Pauline glared at her father: how dare he? He wanted to get rid of her: well, she wanted to get rid of him, too. Silently, with enormous resentment, she handed the bucket to Viv.

'You make your own one. Leave mine alone.'

Viv, mouth trembling, set to work. The two sisters were not exactly competing, but they wanted to do as well as they could. Pauline kept on with the spade, which she had not relinquished, and cut intricate patterns into the sandshapes. With her hands, she patted other shapes in order around them. Her face was gritted with determination: she would enjoy herself, she would.

'I don't know why on earth you forgot the other bucket and spade,' John snapped at Harriet, quietly, so the children wouldn't hear.

'I can't remember everything,' she said mildly. 'Besides, you remembered your book, I remembered the picnic. It wouldn't have been too much for you to remember the bucket and spade too, would it?'

'You're so bloody unreliable. I can't leave anything to you; all you think about is yourself. Your head in the clouds all the time.'

'I can't see any clouds,' said Harriet, smiling as though she pitied him.

John half-spat, and carried on with his book. Harriet looked at her daughters, so beautiful, tanned and healthy, their hair cut short, playing. She didn't take their squabbling seriously; why, at other times, they played together, kissed and hugged each other. She could not help but love them even though she was not sure that they were what she wanted.

She was not sure that John wanted them at all.

And neither she nor John was what the other wanted. There were no longer any illusions about that. It was ten years since they had married. Ten years: it felt twice as long, three times. She despised herself for retreating more and more into herself. Her imagination, always there, always rampant, seemed to have taken over. Life had disappointed her so bitterly. Nothing would be any good now, for what was she good for? She was nearly thirty. All she had left was this, with very little to show, and no one else to share it with.

John wasn't concentrating on his book: he was contemplating his family. He and Harriet had known each other for eleven years, and he dearly wished he had never set eyes on her. She was so untouchable, she didn't care. Not about anything, certainly not for him. Didn't even care that he had slept with other women once or twice. In fact, he thought bitterly, she was probably rather glad. It kept him away from her, didn't it? She wasn't interested in sex, wasn't interested in companionship, in arguing, in life, in anything at all. Everything was up to him. Without him, there wouldn't be this family holiday in Dorset, where they had the good luck to have sun every day. And he didn't just mean the finance, the wherewithal. It was the thought, the desire, everything. She'd have been just as glad for him to take the girls away on his own. Perhaps he'd do just that next year.

But no: he couldn't do that, not really. It conflicted entirely with his image of the family, his family come what may. Besides, what would he do with two little girls for a fortnight? He'd be driven mad. Half the time, he didn't even think they liked him very much.

'Fancy a game of ball, girls?'

Pleasantly surprised, they shrilled: 'Yes, Daddy.'

39

'Can we do it over there?' Pauline said, still whining. 'We mustn't mess up my sandcastle.'

They ran for a few minutes, getting nearer the sea. Harriet, putting on her sunglasses, watched them getting further and further away. Their clear voices came to her from what seemed a great distance. Other sounds came as well, birds, lapping sea noises. She knew she ought to feel happy, her family out there playing, the sun shining, herself watching. But she wasn't: she was alone, incapable of happiness, of involvement.

Come forward a few years. Viv at fifteen – an immature, young-looking fifteen, somewhat too serious, too fond of mooning around in her room rather than going out. Harriet, remembering, worried about that. But still: she had what Harriet had lacked at that age, a quantity of gregarious friends, who would ask her to go out with them to meet . . . boys.

The boys all thought her frozen, at an age when you're very much one thing or another. If you're a girl. But, of course, she was equally dismissive of them, because they didn't match up. She sought someone who was interested in more than how far he could get. Teenage boys very likely wanted to get out of it too, but didn't know how.

Still, Viv found someone who had an idea. Rob. Oh, Rob played the piano, Rob had blond hair, was jibed at for being gay – although he didn't think he was. Sensitive.

Pauline had been going out with Ray for a couple of years by that time, and she was so dismissive, and worldly-wise about it.

'Oh-oh, Viv's caught herself a boyfriend.'

Viv would remain silent, staring, hostile.

'You would get yourself a poofter, wouldn't you?'

'Oh, shut up, Pauline. You don't know anything.'

40

'Don't I just. I've been going out with boys for three years longer than you have. Didn't think you'd ever get one.'

'Well, now I have, so just shut up about it.'

And sometimes Ray would join in.

'Been playing the piano lately, little girl?'

Viv was astounded that Pauline could put up with him.

As for Rob, he turned out to be the male equivalent of that old-fashioned fantasy, a gentleman in the drawing-room, and a whore in the bedroom.

Even their first meeting was intimate. Her friend, Annie, introduced them:

'This is Rob. He lives next door to my aunt and babysits for her sometimes.'

They looked at each other. Viv said: 'And does she pay well?'

They both burst out laughing: Viv out of nervousness, Rob out of amusement at her deadpan expression.

'Very.'

Then someone turned off the lights. It was ten, and the parents might be back soon. There was no time to be lost.

'Oh God,' said Rob, embarrassed and annoyed. This was all too quick. 'Let's go outside.'

They sat on the lawn which, other than them, was solely occupied by elongated bodies.

'Do you know that constellation?' he said. She shook her head, and followed his gaze to the sky. 'Aren't they beautiful?' She nodded slowly, and turned her face to him. He looked quite like her, she thought suddenly: it was his vulnerability rather than any physical characteristic. His eyes were very blue, but childish and round, almost hiding under his feathery fringe. She placed her hand on top of his, and, shutting their eyes, they moved their lips together.

My first kiss, thought Viv as it was happening, and wondered about the suddenness of it all.

'Can I go out with you?' he said, as they separated, Viv wondering whether she had done it properly. She pursed her lips in a tight smile, nervous.

'That would be nice.'

And so it began. Three months of perfect bliss. And

although she knew he was going to join his parents in Canada at the beginning of September, she didn't let that bother her because they were together, and would be afterwards, even if they had to be parted for a while.

Her parents seemed to enjoy it, playing the role of indulgent parents to the hilt. Make sure you're home by this time, that time. Is Rob coming round for tea? How sweet.

They thought her missing him was sweet when he went away, although he would not be coming back. But Viv truly felt that she was being carved up, without anaesthetic. Even when their letters fizzled out she never forgot him.

THE PRESENT

I was wound around with my duvet, very comfortable, not asleep but then I seemed to be sleeping less and less these days. A brush on my face, then air blowing up and down it. I opened my eyes and there was Pauline.

'Hello,' she said. She looked very normal, wore jeans and a T-shirt and her wedding dress in turns. Despite her solidity, her figure had a diaphanous aspect.

'Are you dead?' It was the first thing that came to mind.

She laughed.

'Are you all right?'

She laughed again, sat down on the bed next to me. I was frightened, looked down on the bed for a depression: there was none.

'Don't worry,' she said.

She grabbed my hand, and her touch was warm, human, real. Pauline was coming into my room playing the Virgin Mary, the ghostly maiden, and herself.

'What are you playing today?' I asked.

'Sorry?' she smiled.

'Who are you?'

'Oh, come, come, Viv,' she was laughing at me. 'Don't you recognise me?'

'Pauline,' I said sullenly.

'Look,' she said. 'Don't you worry about me, and tell Mum and Dad not to worry about me either. I'm worried about you, and so should they be. Something's up.'

Now what was this about? I felt better than I had for quite a while.

'How d'you mean?'

'Don't bottle yourself up in your room like you've been doing. Get out into the world and react.'

Bloody typical Pauline, nagging me to do things that she wouldn't do herself.

'Look,' she continued, face fallen, all contrition. 'We're not getting along too well, are we? My fault.'

And she was gone.

Awake, asleep, had she been, had she? Viv didn't know. The red figures on the clock radio seemed to have moved on, and, of course, it had been light for ages.

Oh, oh, oh, oh, oh, oh, oh, don't touch that dial. The radio nudging, then blasting her into the day. Music, trivia, game shows and what she really wanted, almost but not quite more than anything in the world, was a true lover here beside her sleeping body.

Two hours, three hours, four hours, since Pauline had gone.

Now it was time for Viv to go to work, and so she got up obediently, washed, dressed, and went to the station as usual. The passengers seemed astonishingly ugly that morning: monstrous somehow, abnormal.

When she got off the tube, she walked to her office, it was a lovely day, sunny, bright. Viv passed the side of an immense building; she felt strong and good, brave and free.

Then, what was it, she looked down and at regular intervals there were dead seahorses: cracked, ground into the pavement, each with some of its parts missing. What sadness: she could hardly move for it.

Up to the door, and opened. People crossing this way and that, carrying things, all purposeful. One of them said: 'Hello, Viv.' Her mouth responded for her, as she could not, all surprise. Up in the lift, just two floors. It did not take her stomach, that was only when she was going down.

'An early start, eh?'

Going into her office was a big shock. It was empty except for Jean, but other than that its air should have been prosaic.

'It's only eight forty-five,' said Jean, glancing up.

'Yes, I got the early train.'

Viv was surprised that she said that so normally. In fact she felt battered, stunned by normality.

Jean was quiet once more, her hair piled on top of her head seemed to move independently as she looked down at her writing. Such concentration. Viv starerd at her for a few seconds, but not enough for Jean to notice. Or perhaps she was too afraid to notice. That thought bucked up Viv somewhat.

'Can I get you a coffee, Viv?' Jean asked.

'Thanks. Thanks very much.'

Viv glanced down at her typewriter, and noticed a line there. Did I do that? She gasped at it, screwed up her eyes, tried to make sense of it all. So where did that come from, she wondered. I don't remember doing anything with my hands; surely they are still lying in my lap.

She picked up her hands, waved them in and out of focus in front of her face. Her fingers were stubby little numbers, her palms round. They looked slightly yellow, as though marinated in a nicotine solution. The colour faded as you went up the arm.

There was written:

> The quality of mercy is not strain'd;
> It droppeth as the gentle rain from heaven

'Fucking rubbish,' she said aloud, and angrily ripped the paper from the typewriter. It screeched in protest.

A cold flash went diagonally from one corner of her back to the other. Now one part of her body was acting and her brain had not the slightest remembrance of it. Viv hardened her outside shell and took up her work. She said thanks to Jean when she brought her coffee. She lit a cigarette, which she rarely did at work, and began. She, too, could be absolutely normal, could carry on with her work quite superficially, not thinking. She could let her fingers skim over the pages.

'Did you throw away that paper in the machine?' Jean asked. So this was the devil, she could see inside me, there

45

was no escape, perhaps she watched me doing it, laughed as I sat here in turmoil.

'It's just that I'd typed a few lines on it, because I'd had an argument with Ron about that quotation: I looked it up here.'

That night the tube was awful, the train was awful: I had to stand all the way home. There seemed to be little air, and what there was seemed composed of smoke and mustiness. Mine, probably.

It would have to be today that I had to stand, my body was dropping: I was tightening it piece by piece, concentrating as I had to at work, but at least I was sitting then. And I had smoked another packet of cigarettes. It was a way of stilling my hands.

The people, fellow travellers, formed a grey background. It was hard to take them in: just their outline would have to do. Outside the train, patches of forsythia glared amongst the dereliction.

I wasn't mad then.

You'd have thought this idea would reassure me, but no. I thought back over my life and the past couple of weeks, and I was confused. At least in my more manic periods, I thought I was in charge. Now I knew that I was not, and the idea was terrifying.

As I was grabbing at the strap, I noticed a bloke giving me the once-over in an odd fashion. He was wearing a suit, quite a smart one, but his appearance was wild. He had thick glasses and thick hair, which stuck out in a ginger cloud. Truly, he was staring, he was leaning forwards, getting up from his seat:

'Would you . . . ?'

'My station . . .' and I leaped out.

Stupid, stupid.

The walls were high in Viv's room, and the window to the outside long, but the effect was comforting. She was surrounded, at home, with the familiar.

There was a knock on the door, but she heard it with resignation.

'Come in.' She didn't even need to sigh.

'I came to see you. I hope that's OK.'

It was Josh, and Viv was absolutely astonished. She really hardly knew him.

'How are you?'

'Oh, fine, really. And you?'

Silent through nerves, or garrulous through nerves, Viv was now in the unaccustomed position of feeling supremely confident. It was the contrast between herself and this man.

'Well, I'm still pretty depressed after my break up with Linda.'

'Yes, it's a sad thing to happen.'

'You remember, before, she told me I was too clinging.'

Viv nodded.

'Now it's worse. She won't speak to me on the phone or anything.'

He got a ready-rolled joint out of his pocket, and lit it.

'She makes me feel like a complete wanker, but you can't go out with someone for two years, and then not even want to know what's happening to them, can you?'

'No. No, you can't.'

'I mean it's not as though our relationship was terrible. I didn't think so at any rate . . .'

He carried on. And on and on and on. Viv kept looking at his face, smoked a little of his joint, smoked an entire cigarette. She dimly remembered that she had been trying to give up.

And then with one sudden, horrible, certain feeling, she knew that he had become much closer to her. He was looking up at her with a hangdog expression, his eyes rolled pathetically upwards.

'Oh, Viv,' he said, coming closer, putting his arms around her neck. His face came up against her neck and pressed, like an infant rooting for food.

47

'You're such a kind person, I don't know what I'd have done without your support.'

'I've not really done anything,' she said diffidently. He moved his face away from hers.

'You have, you know.'

He stared at her very closely, his eyes wandering around her face.

'I'd very much like to kiss you,' he said, and without waiting for an answer moved in. His tongue felt like a wandering worm in her mouth, but it was astonishment rather than anything else which led her to allow its presence there. Josh pulled away first.

'I'd be so happy if we could sleep together. So happy.'

Damn him, Viv thought. At the same time she was sorting through her mind: how to refuse him without wounding him too badly.

'I'm sorry, Josh. I'm being, like, positively celibate at the moment.'

Christ, she heard herself, she sounded ridiculous.

'In any case,' she continued. 'I've got period pains and no contraception at the moment.'

He looked down at his hands, disappointed, but then it had been worth asking. It always was.

'Oh, well.' He edged towards the door, as Viv looked guilty, and tried to assuage it by saying:

'I hope you feel better soon. Tell me how you get on, OK?'

She showed him to the door and watched him, almost thoughtlessly, as he trailed down the road. Back in her room, she picked up the glass ashtray they had been using and hurled it hard against the wall.

Viv had not seen either of her flat-mates since she had come home from work. Just Josh. What an idiot, his behaviour astounded her. What the hell was he playing at? She looked with amazement at the shattered remains of the ashtray for so long that she thought maybe she was asleep standing up. Her body sagged, her fingers curled, her teeth nagged, her lips pouted unconsciously. She could feel her body set as part of the room; she was part of the furniture. And through her mind passed the recurring vision of Josh – snuggling up to her. It was really hard to believe.

Sheila was sitting, also staring into space, by the kitchen table. Her elbows resting on it, she blew smoke slowly upwards in a nearly vertical stream. She left her lips pursed and stared, following the smoke. Viv wondered in which film she'd seen that, then felt that rather unfair. Presumably Sheila was reflecting on her new lover.

'Hi.' Viv had slipped in quietly, and Sheila looked at her with surprise and, she suspected, disdain. She pulled up the chair and sat down, picking a match from the ashtray, and dissecting it.

'Good day?' asked Sheila.

'So-so.'

Viv carried on picking at the match. When it could be split no longer, she picked another one.

'The oddest thing just happened to me,' she said. 'Josh came over for my sympathy and propositioned me.'

Sheila roared with laughter.

'So that's what he was after. I saw him come round, and wondered what he wanted.' She shook her head, smiling.

'But I hardly know him.'

'Since when has that mattered? He's a bit of a philanderer.'

'Why me?'

'Maybe he fancies you,' Sheila said. 'Maybe he thinks you'd be a soft touch because you've been sympathetic. I've always tried to avoid him myself.'

'Or maybe he thinks because there's no one on the scene that I ought to be grateful. Honestly, the way it happened.'

She related it.

'What a creep. Still, I feel a bit sorry for him,' said Sheila when Viv had finished.

'You'd feel sorry for anyone.'

'I certainly would not.' Sheila laughed again.

As Viv went to fetch some food, they discussed who should be delegated to clean the filthy oven. Then they lapsed into silence once more, Viv thinking that soon, soon, she ought to go to bed whatever time it said on the clock. Once more, for the umpteenth boring day in a row, she would have to get up and go to work.

'Look, Viv, as a friend, what is the matter with you?'

Now this was sudden. Viv swallowed. Of course, this was what she had been avoiding, the reason she had stuck herself in her room night after night, unable to face Sheila and Eric. And now, she was called upon, had to speak, to say nothing was to speak none the less. She opened her mouth, but no sounds came out. She tried for the second time, gasping in plenty of air, which went straight to her eyes. They were overflowing.

'Oh, Viv.' Sheila got up and sat on the table, next to Viv's chair. She leaned forward, and put both arms around Viv, who showed no signs of speaking. Sheila was fairly accustomed to giving support and solace to weeping women, and occasionally men, but had never found one less responsive. Viv, meanwhile, was deeply embarrassed by her tears, but still they kept on coming.

'Do you want to talk about it?'

Viv shook her head, and composed herself just sufficiently to say: 'I can't, I'm sorry. Not at the moment, anyway. I'm sorry.'

'That's OK.'

But Sheila was annoyed, wanted to know what was going on. She liked, needed, to know what was going on.

'For the moment, I just need some sleep. I didn't get any last night.'

'Oh?'

'I thought someone was in my room.'

Viv got up, kissed the top of Sheila's head, pushed the other chair to, and left the room. She saw Sheila staring at her as at a crazy person, and she laughed inwardly. But that made her feel guilty – after all that kindness and attention. And she had not spoken, not said a single word about Sheila and Jackie, no congratulations, no comments, no questions.

50

Bad. She dragged herself slowly up the stairs. It was nine pm, and she fell asleep on top of the bed with all her clothes on.

She became aware of this at six am, sunk, face down, into the duvet, growingly uncomfortable but not really cold. The sky outside was a static grey. She dozed off to sleep.

An hour later, the dream awoke her. There were a lot of men, crawling all over her, the worm-like feeling. Arms, legs, everywhere. As soon as one noticed her, started touching, others seemed to come from nowhere to cling to her body. Periodically, these grasping hands and foraging mouths remembered her existence.

'Oh, don't you just love it all ways at once, baby.'

It was a statement, not a question, and then one man ejaculated all over her left shoulder.

'It would be a shame to waste it,' said one, sidling up to her as she lay on a cushion, legs open as she had been left. This one, it seemed, came from Phoenix, Arizona. In a trice, Viv could feel him begin to thrust, his after-shaved cheek against her nose. A strange hand began to feel its way up her flank:

'Lovely pussy, lovely lady, lovely fuck.'

Her whole body shook with one enormous laugh: it welled up in her eyes, made her shout. The man thought passion was making her groan and came at once.

In the last part of the dream she was violently sick. She could still feel it in her mouth when she awoke again, unrefreshed, to the musical drivel of the clock radio.

Always when it rained at the cottage, Harriet and Marjorie looked towards the ceiling. It had only dripped once, and they had managed, somehow, to repair the roof afterwards; but still, they looked at the slightly sagging plaster with a tinge of despair.

Today, the roof seemed safe, but the window-sills gave cause for doubt. There were some traces of wet rot but you just had to shut your eyes to it.

It rained on and on, in that permeating, inescapable way it seems to in the poorer parts of the countryside. It battered against the windows.

'Don't worry, I'll clean the bath out soon.'

Marjorie was painting her toenails, sitting on a kitchen chair, her feet on the table. Her toenails were muted purple, painted in three deft strokes.

'It doesn't matter. I didn't mean to be snappy.'

Harriet was making flapjacks. She poured a great quantity of oat flakes into a pan and stirred. The rectangular cake tin was ready. Then it was all in the oven, and she was clearing up.

'I'll do it anyway,' said Marjorie. 'It needs it.'

She wiggled her toes.

Harriet sat, looking helpless.

'We've talked so much about this . . . situation,' she said. 'I feel so tired of it all. I don't seem to be able to get off to sleep any more. Thoughts invade my head nineteen to the dozen.'

'Try some herb tea tonight. Honestly, it's worth a go, isn't it? Even if it doesn't taste too great.'

'OK, maybe I will. But there's still all day to get through.'

Marjorie put her arms around Harriet for a few moments, and Harriet responded. Then they separated, went about their various chores.

As she went towards the door, Marjorie said: 'Days like today, rain and housework, always remind me of old Malcolm. I suppose it's because housework's what I remember most about my marriage: he'd come in, make a mess, and go out again.' She laughed, and shut the door.

Harriet sitting, watching the raindrops trail slowly down the distorted window pane, could smell the flapjacks cooking. A lovely smell. If only the nagging twist at the back of her mind would go away. Yet for those few moments she had forgotten, and guilt came with the remembering. And there was nothing else to be done.

'Time to take the flapjacks out of the oven, lovey.'

'Oh, right.' Harriet had been asleep with her eyes open. 'We'll be eating them soon, I hope.'

'Now, if you like.'

They were a bit sickly and burnt your mouth still, but who cared?

In the early stages of their relationship Harriet and Marjorie had each wondered, initially without telling the other, whether they should make their relationship a sexual one. On a warm, earthy, intense evening, it had nearly become so. But when they talked about it seriously some time later, when a dissatisfaction with their marital sex lives had come into the discussion, they had decided against it. What they had together, as friends, was too valuable to risk; it would be very, very dangerous. This, they decided together. Separately, they were regretful and hoped that it was not a permanent decision. They remembered it now, sitting, silent, edgy and exhausted, at the kitchen table.

Harriet looked around the kitchen, at their parsley gushing freshly out of a terracotta pig, and the red and white striped cups hanging from the shelves; at the row of cookery books which they had bought when considering a small catering business. She put her head down on her folded arms. The table where they rested smelt of ancient onions.

'Look,' said Marjorie, rubbing one hand against the other. 'I have this feeling. I know she's all right. Pauline is all right. I can tell.'

Harriet tried hard to refuse a favour offered with difficulty.

'Thanks, Marj, but no.'

'Really, she is all right.'

'Please, no.'

Her heart was beating very quickly, taking her over; she thought maybe her shaking would knock her over. There could be no more of it.

The sickness was still in my mouth and stomach. I was

swimming in it; I was invaded by my dreams. I had wanted to have a bath, but the water was cold. It was part of the conspiracy: it needed me unclean and, as in the dream, I had no choice in the matter. No choice, no choice.

Eric and Sheila were either out or sleeping: perhaps they were avoiding me, but on second thoughts, why should they? That was my forte. Anyway, there was no sign of them. Drank some cold tea, washed myself perfunctorily in cold water, out. It was raining, a steady drip. I didn't have an umbrella so it just came down on me. It's funny how the rain gets to you: the noise, the wet assault, no choice.

Anyway, I'd just boarded the train when my attention was caught by a woman in anorak and jeans. She was wearing a green cagoule, caught up tightly round her face. Her jeans were tight, over heavy thighs, and underneath them were high-heeled boots. I watched her dispassionately. She looked like Pauline, but not enough for me to think that it was her. She stopped on the platform, did not bother to get the train, as though she was waiting for someone. She spun around on one heel, this woman, displaying a brown, satchel-type bag, and then she exaggeratedly stepped: heel, toe; heel, toe. Then she spun around again.

Her eyes burned in her face: they were a strange, intense green. She stared at me, and stared, trying to tear me apart. It wasn't a stare of hate, it was of accusation, of fault, of blame, of pity, of sadness. I looked around at my fellow passengers, to make sure that I was the recipient of all this; none of the rest of them even looked up.

I looked up again. She was still staring, still staring, as we moved off; doing the occasional spin as I sat back. She looked quite like Pauline. Quite like her, not enough. But she was enough to disturb my trip.

Up, out, slam the door against the side of the train. Many people leave the doors open, but it's much tidier shutting them. Then out of the barrier, straight ahead, down the escalator, banging shoulders on the tube.

And after a few anxious looks, craning my head this way and that past all those strap-hangers, men in suits, I was safe. The tube chugged slowly through the stations, discharging and ingesting, full of cardboard cut-outs. Half the time, I felt like a cardboard cut-out. And the other half: well, every cell in my body seemed twice as alive, as though it was going to burst out of my skin. It never gave me any warning as to which it was going to be.

So I heaved myself up out of my seat and pushed out from the crowd, with many excuses because at least I try to be polite. Going up the escalator, I could feel something, a feeling in the back of my neck. Bothersome, unidentifiable.

Out. The fresh air was, as usual, a bit of an assault, stinging my eyes, catching my throat, even though it was only vaguely damp now and not at all cold. Up the road a little, I turned around for a final check and there, in the distance, just emerging from the open mouth of the tube, was the strange, spinning woman. Her hair was loose now, blonde; it looked familiar and suspicious.

She was striding up the road towards me with wide, heavy strides. Purposeful: she was out to get me. As I quickened my pace, so she quickened hers. She was catching up, she seemed to get quicker and nearer and my office was still miles away. Indeed, I seemed no nearer to it at all. I suddenly began to run: taking off, not looking to see whether she was still following. It was hard, and although I was making running movements, was in fact running, it was as hard as swimming in a dream.

But this was not a dream and I did get to my office. Rushed cold, sweaty, through the door and into the lift, and into the office. I dashed to the window, and surreptitiously looked out from all angles. She was nowhere to be seen, and our doorman would never let in anyone he didn't know, would he?

John hated sleeping alone, although he had often done so before Penny came along. It was at night that he was at his most vulnerable – perhaps everybody was. It was a pretence, he realised; the presence of human flesh merely masked his aloneness, but the feeling was authentic enough for him not to care. He put his arm around Penny's stomach and pulled himself close, nuzzling his head into the back of her shoulders. No replying movement, no sign of attention. But at least she was there.

John had never much liked his son-in-law. It was partly his obsequious manner, partly the usual oedipal stuff between fathers and daughters. John remembered the hunted look in Ray's eyes when they were first introduced. He despised that. But determined teenagers set to make their way were more than a match for him, and Pauline wanted him so much, what was there to do but bow down?

The memory came back to him from some six months ago: it was autumn, at any rate. John had been on his way to work, waiting at the lights, when in the mirror he noticed Ray coming down the steps of an old house with a raised ground floor. He was followed by a woman with bouncy red hair, older than Pauline, probably in her late twenties. They seemed to be having an intense conversation, both of them looking at the pavement, but as they turned the corner they burst out laughing.

Of course, they were having an affair, but how to prove it? John was stuck at the traffic lights, hooted at by drivers behind him. He turned the corner, but they had disappeared.

He carried on to work, puzzled. But after all, it was Pauline's life, and he wasn't going to disrupt it. He didn't have the right. In any case, what if it was something innocent?

Now he was sure it was something else, something sinister. How had he forgotten about it? He looked for the answer in the shadows of the room.

I went to the cinema after work.It was an early evening show in one of those smallish cinemas, where even the people seats away seem to be practically in your lap.

I'd been thinking that I wasn't making the best use of being in London. I knew that life was going on somewhere, but I didn't know where, or what it was. Everywhere people seemed to be enjoying themselves, getting on with life, but they were doing it outside my reach.

I started watching *Frances*. I don't mind admitting it scared me shitless.

This young woman started off full of life and things happen to her so she ends up with all her character gone. It was not that she was reduced to a cabbage, but all her imagination, her capacity to enjoy life, all went.

This could be me if I don't get a hold on myself, if I'm not lucky, if I carry on being outside life as I am at the moment. God, it was so depressing. What made me think I'd want to see something like that with Ray hanging over my shoulder? I was hurting myself on purpose. All the time geting mixed up in things with which I can't cope. So.

Home: it was like being welcomed into something warm, like a gas-fire advert. From the closed kitchen door, I could hear murmurs of laughter, and my chest felt a bit tight. From behind, I was given a big push towards the door, as though someone was thrusting me forwards. My arm moved on strings, to open the door.

They looked up at me, surprised, as though I was a burglar or something. Just Sheila and Eric both sitting, gazing up at me in shock as though I didn't belong there, too. Their conversation stopped.

'Hello, Viv, been out?' Sheila was the first to collect herself.

'Yes,' I said calmly. 'I've been to the pictures.'

'Anything good?' said Eric. I noticed rather uncharitably that his fingernails were thick with dirt. Of course, he worked in the park, but that didn't stop him washing. I bit back the desire to say 'dirty fingers' and instead said: '*Frances*. Do you know it?'

They actually glanced at each other, I could see them.

'That's about Frances Farmer, isn't it?'

'Yes, it was really depressing.'

(What Sheila and Eric saw before them was a small young woman, hair standing on end, looking as though she might cry at any moment. Viv embarrassed them, but they couldn't let someone just fall to pieces on the premises. How long had she been like this? It was hard to say: sometimes it seemed as if it had been going on for as long as they'd known her. But then her previous good humour would come back and they could forget their worries.)

'Why, Viv?'

'Why what?'

'Why are you acting like this? Don't you see, you must help us to help you.'

If this situation had been drawn as a cartoon, it would have shown vivid colour sweeping over a character from head to toe. Over me.

'How am I acting?' The voice came out rather sqeaky, and even I could hardly hear it. Their eyes met. Odd, because I had always thought that they didn't get on very well.

'It's just . . .' Sheila looked uncomfortable, but this made me feel affectionate: it must be hard.

'You seem to be very withdrawn suddenly, to sort of dash off to your room.'

(Anger, I thought: what was wrong with that?)

'A bit, perhaps,' I said meekly. I didn't want to talk about it with Eric there. I tore up a cigarette paper, shredding it diagonally. 'I'll try,' I continued, but their disapproving expressions told me that wasn't quite the right answer.

Suddenly, I heard a bang, and in came Jackie, eyes glowing, to plonk down a bottle of wine in the middle of the table.

'Oh, hello there, Viv. How are you?'

What a wonderful woman; my humanity was restored.

'OK, OK, what about you?'

'Well, temping's usually boring, and this job's not the best thing I've ever done, but at least it's racist-free! That beats last week at any rate.'

I wanted to get to her, past that invisible wall between us. She was so different from me and I loved that, I loved it. I wanted to know all about her life. So far I knew almost nothing, and I didn't know how to find out.

'Secretarial work has its moments.'

'Not when I do it, it doesn't.'

'Let's open the bottle, eh?' said Eric cheekily. I always felt Eric put it on a bit, the sweet-little-boy number, when for much of the time he was very bad-tempered. He stretched over the table towards me and grabbed the corkscrew. There were hairs clustering thickly round his watchline. He poured out a glass for me, and I turned it round in my fingers, twisting the stem around and around, its smoothness sending sensual shivers up my finger and arm.

'This bottle's not going to last very long; we ought to have bought another,' said Sheila.

I'm not going to drink any more, I'm too tired,' I said.

'Oh, come on, Viv, don't be silly,' said Jackie kindly.

'No, really, I'm exhausted.' And I coyly sipped the wine. It was red, harsh, and I could feel my insides pickle as it went down. Give me gin any day, but I suppose the money didn't run to it.

'We ought to make our own wine,' said Sheila. 'It's not at all bad to drink, and you can make it from a tin.'

'No, when I want it, I want it now,' said Jackie, and we all laughed. She had a feel for it: she said the right thing, and everyone laughed. Also, she had Sheila; the two of them were together. I wondered what Eric thought.

'You lucky woman, you can get it, too,' said Eric. And laughed again.

'I had never pictured you as being interested in that sort of thing,' I said. Eric looked at me most strangely, with no small degree of shock, and pain filled his eyes. At that moment I realised that he fancied me. God, what a thought.

'Everyone's interested,' he said.

'Perhaps.'

From the silence that followed, I inferred that not only was Eric after me, but that Sheila and Jackie knew this.

'I'm off to bed. Goodnight,' I said.

Getting ready for bed, in the blessed silence of my bedroom, several things preyed on my mind. First, Jackie. Why had I never before paid her much attention? She had not treated me like an outcast, but like the ordinary person

I seemed to them all about ten days ago. Then there was Eric and his horrific secret. Surely I was not wrong, nor egocentric. I had never seen such a look from Eric before, it was really odd. What was he doing fancying me anyway, how dare he? But I knew I was being silly. It wasn't his fault.

And at the back of my mind, then the front, then taking over completely, was that film, that damned film. There was no danger of that, no danger at all.

'Well, what do you think? Should we do something?'

Sheila, impatient, looked at Jackie. She was worried, but it wasn't always easy to pin down exactly what was the trouble.

'Short of really extreme measures, there isn't anything you can do, is there? Anyway, she just seems a bit quiet to me. Quieter than usual.'

'But you haven't seen her, Jackie, when she's all confused and looks at us as though we shouldn't be here.'

'She's somewhere else,' said Eric.

'Well, that's no reason for intervention,' said Jackie. 'And I'm still not sure whether you're totally over-reacting. She was acting fine when I talked to her, and I'm sure it was because I was talking to her like a normal person.'

'But that's because she's never behaved like this before, and over the past few days it's got worse and worse.'

Sheila leaned back in her chair and swigged the remainder of her wine. She smiled at Jackie with her eyes, but her lips were still pressed hard together.

'Do you think she's having a breakdown?' Eric said.

'I've got about as much idea as you have. Nervous breakdowns aren't that easily classifiable; people act in different ways. Anyway, two years as a student nurse doesn't make me a psychiatrist.'

'No, but you are outside this household so have a different perspective from us,' Eric continued.

'Have you contacted her parents; maybe they should know?'

'We don't really want to do that,' said Sheila.

Conversation lapsed and then, as if rehearsed, the two women got up, said goodnight, and disappeared from the kitchen. Soon, Eric could hear the soft sounds of Aretha Franklin coming from Sheila's room. Lucky them, he thought.

Earlier in the evening, Eric had felt quite exuberant: he'd gone that afternoon to the travel agents to book a flight to America. It would be something different, and his life had become monotonous.

Once, Eric had had a girlfriend who called him the bear. Eric was a large man, with a beard, and long arms and legs. She called him the bear either when they were having sex or when he was upset about something. Wendy, her name was; where was she now, he wondered? Their parting had been acrimonious.

He felt bearish just now: huge and lumbering and hairy. He stretched his arms out, staring at them, examining them. Then he drew back his hands and pressed them to his face; pressed the tears back into his eyes and, when they escaped, he pressed them into his cheeks.

Harriet's dreams were full of Pauline's and Ray's house. She was in it, staying in it; she was outside, looking at it. The modernity of it, the sheer newness of its evil struck her again and again. So things did not have to stretch back, she thought to herself in the dream. They could just start.

By the end of the dream, Harriet was living in the house. She was unsure if she had bought it, or whether she was just a long-term guest. Then one day as she was watching television she realised that it had become irredeemable, entrenched with evil, and she had to get out. But she couldn't leave the room, and had to stay there until someone came back. The television played on and on, comedy programmes appeared at which she tried to laugh, but no one came. No one, no one, and all the time the walls got closer and closer together, until she could almost feel them except she was sure they hadn't moved. The terror of that awoke her.

For a split second she thought that she was still married and that John's sour body was lying next to hers. The realisation that she was alone was almost as frightening as the dream had been. Then she looked around the ceiling, and the moonlight flickering in through the windows, with their lead-diamond panes, and her stomach contracted. Something seemed to be getting in the windows, a frosty, misty feeling, like a black and white horror film. She blinked, and it disappeared.

She cast her eyes over the ceiling, plaster ceiling rose in the centre which gave off lots of tiny shadows, and places where it was quite dark. And the wardrobe with the mirror: she didn't even want to look at that. If only she had shut the curtains – which she never did – then she would not have to suffer this. She clicked on the bedside light.

The light bulb glowed orange through the red shade, reflecting warmth in the mirror which a few seconds ago had menaced. Harriet's bedclothes were in homely lumps rather than concealing folds. Her things piled on the chair were dirty and prosaic. She could have wept with relief.

She turned off the light again and went back to sleep.

On the station again, lurking, that woman. Still wearing a cagoule, although it wasn't raining. She wasn't looking at me: she was hiding in the corner, behind a pillar, shifty. Once I had taken my seat on the train, she came out onto the platform, waving her shoulder bag, twirling it around. She had to get me, had to catch me up, catch me out, she was there. Keeping an eye on me, no doubt.

The solution came after I got to work, before my workmates arrived. I was in the middle of typing some letters for publication about the role of education and whether by concentrating on the GCSE/syllabus, children were missing out on other things. I had one A-level, which I had merely scraped, because I really couldn't care less. The upshot of it was I decided to follow her. She wouldn't expect that, and attack is the best form of defence, they say. It would mean being late for work, but, as I was never late, that didn't matter. I wouldn't even feel guilty about it.

So now it was just a matter of waiting for her to put in an appearance. I waited ten minutes, until just before the others were due to arrive. Going quickly to the window, looking out onto the budding trees below, I tried to find her. Maybe I'd forgotten that she wouldn't be there; she only turned up at the station after all. And I had always missed her, or she me.

'Beautiful outside, isn't it?'

That was Jean, coming into the office, a note of surprise in her voice as, to look out of the window, I had to haul myself over her desk.

'Oh sorry, I don't think I've messed up anything.'

Jean laughed: 'Oh Viv, you're the last person to mess up anything.'

That remark didn't exactly please me, and somewhere I thought: 'If only you knew.' But then the feeling went, and I apologised once again.

'It's such a lovely day today, after all.'

'Like summer.'

'And it will be soon.'

Pauline's wedding was in the summer. All that bloody drunken dancing, all that blossoming hope, like the cherry trees on the way to work. And it never came to anything, just as the blossoms simply dropped off the trees: fading, limp blossoms carpeting the floor, and expectations which could never be fulfilled.

Her marriage was like that: her expectations of it could never amount to anything. My expectations, though, did come true. Could never admit that, could I?

'And the printers are being very slow for September's issues,' Jean continued, and I was surprised to realise she had been talking without my hearing her at all.

'You know,' I said, 'I still find it difficult to remember we go to press so far in advance. At the moment it's spring, and for magazine purposes, it's the autumn.'

'Yes, your life is just wished away.'

Wished. I liked the way she said that, with a kind of swooshing sound. Not that you could say so, of course.

I took one last look out of the window, but she had not appeared, as, of course, she would not. But perhaps if I focused my mind, I could find that woman before she found me.

John believed in taking a rational approach to fear, so that when he awoke in a cold sweat, he tried to persuade himself that it was simply foolishness, brought about by sudden awakening. As his eyes shot open, Penny moved in her sleep towards him, and straightened her legs.

'Penny . . . Penny.'

'Mm.' She turned and put her arms around him, pulling her body in to be embraced.

'Penny, I've had a dream.'

He felt totally lucid, totally awake.

'Martin Luther King,' she said into his neck.

'No, not like that. Wake up a bit, darling.'

He turned on the bedside light.

'What's wrong?' she asked. Only serious talks took place at four am.

'The dream I had, it was extraordinary.'

He folded his hands above his head, half propped up against the bed-head.

'Some of it happened to me before – in real life, I mean. I watched Ray and a woman with floating red hair run down a small flight of steps, deep in conversation. That bit actually happened. Then they got into a car, just in front of the mine, at traffic lights. But the car I was in wasn't mine, it was an old banger. I knew I had to follow them, but my car would never keep up. Still, I could always just see them, and in an eerie street next to a warehouse they stopped. It was desolate, abandoned docks, or something. They didn't see me. Suddenly, I was standing on a wall, looking down on them. They slipped through a rickety door into an open space, dirt and dust surrounded by corrugated iron, where they stood alone, looking up at the grey sky. Still, they couldn't see me. Then they started digging, scrabbling away at the dirt with their bare hands for ages, ages, and then I saw something. It was a hand. It was a hand, dear God, with a finger pointed in accusation. And when they discovered it, they looked up at the sky again and started beating each other with their fists and then they fell onto each other screaming and shouting and crying.'

He lay quietly looking at the ceiling, but pained; Penny lay in silence next to him. He turned to her, nestling his head onto her shoulder for comfort.

'I'm frightened,' he said.

She turned her full attention to him, stroked his hair, and worried, because all this strain was just too much, too much.

'What was that dream trying to tell me?' he continued.

'Well, maybe nothing. Maybe it was just a dream.'

'I don't know,' he continued. 'Until recently, I would have thought that, too. But what with Ray's death and Pauline's disappearance, I'm ready to believe anything. But you have to keep a hold on yourself, even if you can't control what's going on around you.'

She stroked his thinning hair, wispy but still beautifully coloured, tracing the outline of his cheekbones. Penny could feel his pain. She had to get him through it, past the misery, the uncertainty, the fantasy.

65

'I have to be strong,' he went on, 'concentrate on pulling myself together, because Pauline . . .' his voice shuddered, 'because Pauline has to be found. However . . . things have ended up.'

They could hear the soft hum of the off-peak water heating.

'Yes.'

They were quiet once more. Penny's thoughts began to wander, and she was nearly asleep, when John suddenly said: 'That woman, love. What was she doing?'

Penny's eyes shot open again. Oh God, she thought.

'In real life? Perhaps they were having an affair.'

'Maybe they were,' said John with satisfaction.

'But I don't know how you'd discover whether they were. Anyway, the police are probably looking into that. Don't brood, darling,' she said gently. 'Go back to sleep.'

'Yes,' he agreed. 'Yes.' But, the light switched off once more and Penny asleep, John plotted and planned.

Viv came home from work frustrated: the woman had not been there. Of course. Viv had never seen her on the way home, anyway: it was always in the mornings. But still, she was infuriated. She turned her key in the door, ready to shout at anyone who greeted her.

But although there were sounds upstairs, there was no one in the kitchen as she went in to make herself a coffee. Waiting for the kettle to boil, she gazed rather more peacefully out of the French windows leading into the garden. It was quite light still, and the bushes in the garden were almost in leaf. Viv stared and stared at the garden, taking it all in, as though she were rubbing it on her body. It was peaceful, it was growing, and it was nothing to do with her. the thought was very comforting.

She didn't notice Eric come into the kitchen. He stood

silently for a moment and watched her. He felt her calmness, and didn't want to be a disturbance. Suddenly, he experienced great compassion for her and what she had suffered. Over the past days, she had irritated him, but the sight of her sitting there, so peaceful, gazing out of the window made his heart go to her.

'Hello,' he said, still not wanting to break in on her thoughts.

'It's a lovely evening, isn't it?' she said. 'It makes the day worthwhile.'

She smiled at him, a calm, peaceful, beatific smile designed to bestow similar feelings on the recipient.

'Yes,' she said under her breath. They both carried on looking for a while, and then Eric went to the kettle and touched it, withdrawing his hand sharply because it was hot.

'Sorry,' said Viv. 'It's already boiled. I just hadn't got round to making a drink yet.'

Eric began to make tea, and Viv hadn't the heart to tell him that she wanted coffee.

'Sheila's not in tonight,' Eric said. 'She's going out with Jackie.'

'Oh,' said Viv flatly, trying to ignore a twinge of something which made a brief appearance in her stomach.

'Had you decided what to cook tonight?'

Eric spent a while deciding before he came out with this. He had been quite sure that Viv was in no fit state to decide about cooking, and had probably forgotten that such things had to be done. Viv, for her part, did suddenly remember, and was stricken with guilt.

'No,' her voice trailed off.

'Never mind. You know what I really fancy? Fish and chips. Shall I go down and get some?'

'Yes!' The evening, she felt, was getting better. That woman was disappearing from her thoughts.

Eric reappeared very quickly carrying not just fish and chips, but a bottle of cider.

'Oh, Eric, what a good idea.'

He tipped the food onto two plates, and filled two tumblers. 'Cheers!' They smiled at each other over the table, and Eric felt another pang, as Viv lifted her sweet face towards him. Shit, he thought. this is no time to feel that way. And he pushed it to the back of his mind as he had been accustomed to doing for no particular reason. Now, he felt the reason was Viv's sanity and was shocked by his arrogance.

They chatted about the house for a while, and then Viv said: 'Does it worry you that women you know become lesbians?'

Eric blushed, and stared hard at a chip.

'I don't know. Not that many of them have done it.'

Viv wanted to shout at him something about herself, but as she wasn't sure what, she kept quiet.

'Still,' he simpered at her. 'There are plenty of heterosexual women about. I'm not worried yet.'

Viv found it curious the way Eric would suddenly act like a little boy demanding attention, but she didn't entirely dislike it. Probably he felt that if he acted seriously, people would not like him.

'Anyway, what about you, Viv? You haven't been out with anyone for ages.'

'I haven't wanted to, Eric.'

After a few moments' silence, he said: 'Not even Josh?'

'Especially not Josh.'

'Yeah,' said Eric. 'I was just being facetious. He's a bit of an opportunist. Not just with women: he plumps down on the side of what everyone around him thinks at the time, and champions it.'

'But most people do that up to a point. It takes a very brave person to fly in the face of what everyone else believes.'

Eric's face smiled at her over the table. He longed, longed, to ask her what had been the matter, was she all right. But no. He could not do that. She had to trust him.

'For most people it's all compromise, isn't it?'

'Yes, it's all compromise.'

All Viv's life was a compromise, she thought, all the time she was doing things she didn't want to do. And Eric: who knew what she really felt about him? For the moment, he was quite nice really.

'Do you like living here?' he was asking.

'Yes.' She tried to think of places she'd preferred, but there weren't many places at all, and nowhere she could like better than this.

'Yes, it's nice.'

'I like it, too,' he said. 'We all get on fine, and nobody's untidy or anything.'

They both laughed and Viv felt a sudden desire to reach out and touch Eric. It quickly went, and she was grateful that she had not acted upon it.

'Do you know, sometimes I have felt as though I can get anything I want out of life, and at others, recently for instance, it all seems to be drifting out of my reach.'

'Like you don't know what it is anyway.'

'No, no, I don't. Oh, Eric,' she leaned forward towards him, pushing the dirty plate out of the way. 'What is it?' she continued earnestly. 'Sometimes I feel as though I'm not really alive at all, but just going through the motions.'

He was all eyes and ears, all sympathy, trying to live her pain with her. She could not know this, but he had to get to the bottom of what was troubling her.

'But sometimes I do feel in control, you know.'

How, she wondered, could she elicit Eric's help and information without being any more specific?

'I'm not always certain what's happening,' she said eventually.

'No,' said Eric. 'Neither am I.'

Searching around for concrete examples, he said: 'I was always a bit worried about the dynamics between you and Sheila when I first moved in here. You seemed to have this real mother-daughter thing going.'

'I suppose you're right. But we're not like that any more.'

'I'm not close to anyone really,' said Eric. And Viv, in spite of herself, in spite of the fact that she disapproved of men who expended no emotional energy on other men but put it all onto women, felt sorry for him.

'Why not?' she asked.

He shrugged his shoulders, moved about in his bear-fashion, rubbed his jumper sleeves against the table.

'Scared, I suppose.'

They were silent once more, and then Eric said: 'What about you. Who do you talk to?'

She was shocked to realise that, despite casting about in the recesses of her mind, there was no one.

Eric looked at her hard: 'You can talk to me, Viv, if you want.'

They were sitting in the semi-darkness. Viv reached over the table to Eic. As she did it, she realised that she could not remember the last time she had felt true affection for anybody.

'Thank you,' she said.

Still, she could not tell him. She could not allow herself to become more vulnerable than she already was, although he had let down some defences. Instead they remained quiet, drinking, staring at nothing, the red glow of their continually extinguishing roll-ups piercing the darkness.

Was I really on the train, or was it a dream? I couldn't remember how I had got there, but each part of the train seemed to be exact, normal yet threatening. I knew that I was tired: a cumulative lack of sleep turned my blood to lead, and my body into a corpse. Gradually, I could feel myself return to semi-consciousness. No: I definitely was living in real life, rather than a dream world, because there you wouldn't feel you were going to sleep, would you? Well, you might.

'Hey, over here.'

I looked up, but could see nothing.

'Viv, for God's sake.'

It was Pauline, larger than life.

'Eh?'

I could feel my face curl. This was Pauline, Christ, it really was. 'How're you doing?' she smiled. I gawped at her. She was thinner than usual, and she looked ruddy and healthy. Better than she had a few days ago, when I saw her in my room. Or did I? For that matter, was I seeing her now? I lunged forward to touch her, but missed. She shuffled around in her seat, her wavy hair bouncing.

'Don't,' she laughed, but not unpleasantly.

'I don't understand,' I said. 'What are you playing at?'

She looked grave: 'Nothing. There's nothing to play at.'

'This is ridiculous,' I continued, angry. 'Why can't you come back from wherever you are, and stop tormenting everybody?'

'Ssh,' she said. 'Don't let the whole compartment in on the secret. I need to be alone.'

'But you're not being fair on us, we're all desperately worried, don't you know that?'

'Sorry,' she said, annoyed.

'What about Ray?'

'What about him? I want to get away from him and his memory. He's ruined my life.'

'So you destroyed him, eh?'

'No.' She just looked at me, and I thought: she's going to disappear.

'Ray was quite capable of destroying himself.'

'I know.'

At that moment, the doors opened, and many people came into the carriage. They all looked odd, their clothes were somehow not quite right, had been deliberately put together to clash. My attention was distracted for a moment, and when I re-directed my thoughts to Pauline, she had gone.

My disappointment, and then my anger choked me, because whether this really was Pauline, or my imagination, or her in some spirit form, it was really pissing me about when I needed peace, peace. I was not sure whether I was awake or asleep; or mad, sane or simply confused.

I was still there, sitting and brooding and scarcely awake, when we clanged and jerked into the station. I looked up, and there she was, the blonde woman, poking her head above the seat, staring at me. I knew no more: I ran.

Marjorie had no particular routine for her clairvoyance: it just happened. There were ways of nudging it along: sometimes, she sat and concentrated very hard; sometimes, she used her dreams. At other times, she took a long walk and looked at the stars. But this was different: this time, she had a burning desire to know, a feeling that this was meant, coupled with the intense opposition of Harriet. They sat locked over it, not speaking, two sets of elbows on the kitchen table, stuck.

Marjorie was quiet. Of course: one's daughter missing, son-in-law dead, of course you'd be tormented.

'I'm having bad dreams and . . .'

Harriet tailed off. And what? She wasn't sure, perhaps it was nagging guilt that she should have done more, ought to have been able to help, ought to have. And hadn't. She had been a good mother of small children, but adults were different.

'It's just that I might be able to help.'

'And you might make matters a whole lot worse,' said Harriet abruptly.

Eventually she said: 'I'm too frightened. No more, please, Marjorie.'

There was silence. Harriet did not tell Marjorie about her dream: that would make it too real. Even after daybreak the creepy feeling had remained. She woke up feeling shadowed, and had not been able to shake it off. And there was nothing to put her finger on.

Marjorie, on the other hand, had decided to do it without Harriet. She was a little unsure of the ethics, it wasn't just Harriet who would benefit. Natural justice demanded it.

'I'm sure Pauline's still alive,' she said.

'Are you?' Harriet allowed a slip of interest to show. Although what Marjorie was saying did not reassure her, any little flicker of hope was welcome.

'I could delve, Harriet. I could try to go further.'

'Not just at the moment,' Harriet said firmly.

The trouble was, she had nothing to do, nowhere to go, no reason or opportunity to further her own investigations. Despair moved her, or rather didn't, because she knew that even physical movement was pointless. She had to sit and wait.

She got up to stare out of the window: it was a reasonable day, cloudy but with a little sun poking through the gaps.

'You know,' she said to Marjorie. 'I am so full of clichéd feelings, such as why should we still be alive when others aren't.'

She gripped tightly onto the window-sill, unnoticed tears travelling down her cheeks. The sill was slightly gritty, and as she lifted her fingertips to examine the grime left there, the tears turned into sobs.

'I don't think I can take much more of this.'

'I know, I know.'

Marjorie held Harriet's wet face to her shoulder.

'How about if we used a little of my intuition, and some private detection?'

'I suppose anything's worth a go,' said Harriet dubiously.

'That's the spirit, dear.'

Doing something, anything, was better than nothing. But this time it was Marjorie who had the misgivings.

Viv stopped when she got to the telephones, and joined in the queue. She tried to blend in with the people, look as though she belonged. It was hard: she felt so conspicuous. The temporary feeling of release was just that. She wasn't safe yet. She was waiting for the woman, waiting for her to show herself so that Viv could take the initiative and trail her. Now all that was ruined: Viv realised she had been fooling herself. She was scared, cowardly and panicking. That woman had stared at her so strangely, had been there for no evident reason. It was cause enough to be frightened.

When it was Viv's turn to use the phone, she fiddled with it as though unable to get a connection and then stepped to one side, lurking as though she might try again later. Streams upon streams of people were discharging from the trains. People, red-faced men in bowler hats to little kids in tatty uniforms, came close to her and viewed her with suspicion. Did she look crazy, she wondered? The thought cheered her: surely if she really was crazy, then she could never have entertained the possibility. Then again, the ceiling pressing closer and closer to her head made her wonder.

Viv looked up at the clock: yes, it was nine, so she had to have been there quite a while. There were so many people that she was never going to spot her prey amongst them. She should go to work, or at least move, before someone came to get her. As she was contemplating the safety of movement, a youngish man in a neatly cut suit approached her:

'Here, love. Someone wants to speak to you.'

Viv took several deep breaths, trying to satisfy her pulsating solar plexus. She dragged her nails through her hair, firmed her knees, which were proving recalcitrant. Looking around, she saw no one.

'Who?' she said warily.

'Oh, there's a nice gentleman who wants to have a word.'

Viv was curious. Was this someone to come and hospitalise her, or what? She thought: I'd better go quietly, not make a fuss, don't want anyone to notice. Then: perhaps it's her. She's sent a man to get me. What to do? Just go out, she decided, because in the forecourt of Charing Cross station, nobody could really do anything.

A smart man with set blond hair was looking forlorn, still, in the middle of people moving around him in divided waves. He glanced briefly at Viv as she was brought out to him.

'No,' he said sadly. 'That's definitely not her.'

Oh, someone missing, Viv thought, and at that instant said: 'Someone missing?'

'Yes,' he said, and moved off.

Viv felt tremendous sympathy. His overcontrolled manner made her pity him, and his disappointment. She wanted to cry out: 'I'm sorry. I'll be her if you like.'

But she remained silent.

The two men walked off towards the Strand, the younger one putting his arm casually about the elder's shoulders.

74

Comfort, she thought, which was so hard to find. She had an idea where she could go to get it if she wanted, if she only wanted it enough, but it was too scarey.

This would be the turning point, she decided: she would get herself in order and progress to work. She felt as though she had been up for weeks. Her legs were sinking into the ground, she could not stand up any longer. How was it, then, that she was still moving? The lights were glaring, hundreds upon hundreds of them, everything combined to give her a migraine. And the people, hundreds upon hundreds of them, all running, going quickly, making their way in life whereas she wasn't. Hurrying, hurrying. She must keep going, an alien amongst all the normals. And there were those two men again, both slight but tall, lurking at the bottom of the escalator. They stood apart, conferring closely with each other, not seeming even to notice her existence. Why not, she thought irrationally? Was she not important? Nobody else was looking at her either, and this was bothering her. Aren't I collapsing, she thought, aren't I looking like a mad woman?

Every time she stopped acting like a maniac, she sank into torpor. Just waiting, waiting for the tube, not sure whether or not one had come past.

The walls curved inwards, coming at her: a beautiful symmetry, both sides like that. Now, a tube was coming, and she must get on, step right down inside and stand as far as Tottenham Court Road, propped with all the others against a glass panel, not able comfortably to hold all those dangling appendages. The men got on the tube, not noticing her, looking only at each other. This depressed Viv even more: she kicked the panel viciously, once, twice. On the third time, a middle-aged woman said: 'Would you mind not doing that?' This was such a shock that Viv stopped, but hissed down her nose: 'Why?' Instead, she sneakily kicked the panel with the back of her heel until it was time to get off.

She dragged herself slowly, slowly up the escalator and the stairs to the road. It seemed to get steeper every day, the continual redecorating and scaffolding making it even more claustrophobic. How could she get to the office, how make her way up the road with all those other people? Viv was stuck. And she wasn't sure if she was moving either. Maybe a couple of inches. Every step seemed like an age, an enormous lifting of a dead weight. Yet she had to continue: there was nothing she could do where she was and they were expecting her.

'Psst.'

Viv looked around, but there was no one, nothing that could have made that noise. Only people: hundreds and hundreds of them, all undistinguishable, undistinguished. Not like her, still surrounded by that ring.

'Psst.'

There it was again, a sound which could have come from anywhere. It crept up on her. Her head spun from left to right, trying to detect it. And still, she just saw people, hurrying more quickly than ever. Now the rain, hissing and spitting down, seemed to dissolve them. Suddenly there were no more people: the grey sky had despatched them inside. But the noise was still there.

She plodded on, lifting each limb heavily, till she came to a shop. Then, abruptly, she dodged behind a lamp-post. It was that woman, buying some cigarettes, and she had not been noticed. Great. Immediately, she felt strong again; it did not matter that she could hardly move before. Now she certainly could. You bet she could, she could run after that woman and trail her for miles until she found what she wanted. She stayed behind the lamp-post, breathing heavily, excited and exultant. Occasionally, she peeped out to see whether the strange woman had emerged but really she was relying on intuition.

At precisely the right moment, Viv turned at right angles and, keeping next to the wall as she had seen in the films, ducking into doorways from time to time, she shadowed the woman. It was great fun, ducking and weaving, dipping into doorways and popping behind lamp-posts. Up and down, in and out, behind her all the time, praying that she didn't turn round. She didn't. But she walked a hell of a long way, round and round the back streets until Viv was quite lost,

76

running to keep up, the strange woman going so fast, straight along the pavement, no zigzagging, no dipping and diving, just straight along to her destination. Determined. She was formidable, striding forth and conquering the world. Viv had a hard time keeping up with her.

Then she stopped abruptly and turned into a mews. Viv watched her, peering around the corner, as she walked up to one of the pretty little houses, took out a key and opened the door. It was the usual style mews: white cottages born out of stables, now comprising garages and studios below, flats on top. All the cottages had window-boxes with lively spring flowers trailing from them. And the quiet was deathly: it was hard to believe you were in central London. Looking down to the bottom of the mews, Viv could see that there was no way out. Trapped, if she went in; having accomplished nothing, if she didn't.

She sat on the pavement at the entrance to the mews for a while. God alone knew what was the time: they must have been ringing her at home for hours, wondering what had happened. Did jobs ring police stations and hospitals if you didn't arrive? Could someone possibly be at home to worry about her as well?

Viv picked up a matchstick from the gutter, and bent it back and forth until it broke. It was ages since she had had a cigarette, but wasn't she giving them up? She couldn't remember. Fumbling through the pockets of her jacket and handbag, she found a rather crushed packet and lit one. It tasted excellent, and she spat the smoke into the air. The rain, coming down in a drizzle, hit the back of her hands. Viv felt quite adrift from the rest of the world, adrift from what normal people were doing.

What was going on back there, she wondered? What was that woman doing? She had to find out. Like Sherlock Holmes. Very like Sherlock Holmes, because it was quiet and British and didn't seem to involve vice or drugs rackets or violence. A difference from Ray and everything, which she had conveniently forgotten, wanted to forget. She picked up another match and once again destroyed it. Viv was afraid. She hauled herself up off the kerb, and hit herself a few times to get rid of the dust and dirt.

There was a large metal knocker on the door, which was wooden, and finely carved with fancy swirling patterns and a number: seventeen. What the hell. She knocked, and the ornate knocker made a hollow, metallic sound which told of emptiness within. Viv was so certain of that emptiness that when the door opened she nearly fell over.

'Come in,' the woman said. 'I must say we've been expecting you.'

Close up, she was much older than Viv had thought: verging on forty, possibly. She wore tight jeans and a white sweater, which rolled forward at the neck. Her fine blonde hair, stood out slightly with static. She held the door open for Viv, who stepped, with just a little trepidation, over the threshold.

'Why don't you come and sit down,' she said in a kind, relaxed voice.

The hallway was white, with a few dark-framed pictures on the walls. Viv couldn't catch what they were. There was a low ebony chest, and a maroon rug, with brightly coloured patterns on it. The hall led through to a room, also white, with sunlight streaming into it. Had the sunlight been imported, Viv wondered? It had been raining and grey outside, and there had been no time for it to brighten up. There were plants inside and out: large, leafy ones, but without any flowers. These, instead, were in a pale yellow vase on a wooden table, next to the sofa where Viv was motioned to sit down. Viv was simply puzzled: Then, she could hardly believe her eyes.

Another woman, slighter than the first, with more hair, entered. She was carrying a tray, with two flasks and a jug of something orange – juice, Viv thought. She placed it on the table, and raised her eyes coquettishly to look at Viv. The two women were near as damn it clones. Apart from that slight physical difference, they were the same. They wore identical clothes, too.

'It's a pleasure,' the second woman said, and Viv was shocked to hear that her voice, too, could have come from the mouth of the first strange woman. She then sat next to her, and Viv could feel her presence, smell her. She smelled sweet.

'We've been concerned about you, Viv,' she said 'You've been worrying too much, taking too much on board, blaming yourself.'

Viv could scarcely believe it. These women, that she had never seen before: how dare they? Her mouth opened.

'Be a bit nicer to yourself,' the first one continued. 'Because even when you feel you're being self-indulgent, you're still hurting yourself. You know that when you really think about it.'

Viv looked across from one to the other. They really were so alike it was appalling, but with about twenty years between them, Viv now considered. Outwardly, they were comforting her, all very kind and nice, but there was something not quite right.

'How can you do this to me?'

'We're trying to save you from yourself.'

'Good God, you sound like my parents.'

'Perhaps in some ways we are.'

Viv snorted: she was pissed off with them, too. She had hoped to find out something about Pauline, and they had offered nothing, just this nonsense.

'I'm going,' she said angrily, and stood up. As she did so, the door opened, and a number of other women poured into the room. They all smiled at her, with friendly curiosity. She was astonished to see that one of them, perhaps metamorphosised that way or perhaps that way to begin with, was Jackie.

'Viv,' she said warmly.

'Jackie, what's going on here, I don't understand at all.'

'Oh, Viv, don't worry. 'She put her arm round Viv and held her. 'We all want to help you, that's all.'

Viv was conscious of Jackie, of her arms around her. They felt solid.

'Viv.' Jackie held her out at arm's length, so that they were staring each other in the eyes. They were almost exactly the same height and size, although Jackie was the more athletically built.

'I'm not your fantasy woman, you know. I'm real. Just in the same way as you are. Feel.'

She squeezed Viv very tightly, and Viv nodded. Tears began to roll down her face.

'Here,' Jackie said, and handed Viv a neatly folded pink handkerchief. Viv pressed it to her eyes, and put her hand on Jackie's shoulder.

'I don't deserve it,' Viv said.

'What are you talking about? Everyone deserves it. We all hurt, and we all go wrong. I'm not absolving you, I'm just saying that it's all right. You're no more wicked than anybody else.'

Viv's tears flowed yet more heavily at this and she felt she must get away. She turned her back on the brightly-lit garden, and instead headed for the front door which, contrary to her fears, opened quite normally.

It was still grey and drizzling outside; nothing had changed. She walked slowly to the end of the mews, looking round at the cottage. Nothing appeared to be moving in it. No women were looking out of the windows, or climbing onto the roof in an effort to stop her. But there was an atmosphere of un-naturalness, of which she had to rid herself. She needed to be away, far away, back to normal. She ran – around corners, up allies and streets she didn't recognise until she came to a wide open road full of cars. Modern buildings were on each side of the street, but again not many people. Since she left Tottenham Court Road, there had been few people on the streets. Here, she could see people on the other side of the road, but that was far away and she would have to cross a complicated pelican crossing to reach them. And for the moment, the cars whizzed past.

She hurried down the road. She knew it was down: it seemed to be the way people were walking. But it got her nowhere. At the end of it, she just saw an enormous cross-roads, and at the other side of the road another little maze of streets. But reaching the pelican crossing was difficult. It was worth it: take a chance and cross the road, dodging the cars. She ran, she nipped, as the cars swished past. And she had just got her left foot onto the kerb at the other side, when a tremendous force pushed her down onto the pavement and the grey of the sky overcame her consciousness.

Eyes open quickly, blink, all too sudden. What's going on? The ceiling comes and goes, comes and goes, all very rhythmic, but it's going to engulf me. It does.

The next time I open my eyes, it doesn't engulf me any more, but the dead weight on my body allows for no movement, no reaction, eyes staring at the ceiling, at the greyness out of the window, nothing.

Then there is the remembrance: I was knocked down by a car; and the other remembrances: those women, Jackie. I can't believe it. But when I try to get up, try to move any part of my body I can't.

So what? Try to sleep, try to forget that this has happened to me, because it has, and there is no way I can believe it was a dream, or that I hallucinated it. For clutched firmly in my right hand is the pink handkerchief Jackie had given me – tangible evidence. And yet, and yet, I don't really believe it. Not really.

But it's still all out of my control, a puzzle. Forces are taking over my mind and my life, perhaps without even knowing it. What are they anyway?

Sleep, sleep, try to sleep. Safer to seek oblivion than endlessly to turn over all the possibilities in your mind. Not sure whether I can move yet, move at all, ever. Don't know. But I can feel the whole of my body, quite excruciatingly – every bruise and cut. Can't see them though, covered as I am from head to foot in clothes and then bed clothes (who put me here?). I ought to feel hot. I don't, but I can feel dampness around my nose, which I think is sweat. Perhaps it's rain. Perhaps it's tears.

81

I am aware of a yucky feeling, a pain, a boring deep into my stomach. I laugh: I can still do it, I can. The sound comes from deep within my stomach. Perhaps this can persuade me to move. I try. Nearly, nearly. Perhaps later. I try again. This time more nearly.

I was feeling increasingly sticky. What a time to start your period. Yet it cheered me, because some part of my body was still functioning normally. A dissipation of tension, despite the pain digging deep inside me. An ebbing feeling, that it was all slipping out of me, and I had to clear it up.

And up! I sprang, surprised at myself, but the effort of that sent me reeling back onto the bed again. I could move. Thank God. I went into the bathroom, peeled off my clothes, and got into the bath. It was good, and by some miracle I could no longer feel the cuts and bruises. Then clean, undressed, I got into bed.

The expected bang on the door was quite late in coming: six fifteen.

'Viv, are you there?'

I opened my mouth, and just a squeak came out. The door opened and in rushed Sheila:

'Viv, what's going on? You've made such a mess of the bathroom, there's stuff everywhere.'

I smiled at her, sorry, not knowing what to say. I grabbed her hand, squeezed it, I think, and sank back onto the bed.

'Sorry,' I whispered.

She looked aghast at me, terrified as no doubt my appearance warranted. Me, I was a reality, a conundrum she had to solve.

'Jackie,' she yelled, still holding my hand. 'Come here quickly.'

I froze. I didn't know what to make of this. I didn't want to see Jackie, go away, go away. I could hear the sounds of her bounding up the stairs.

'Look at Viv,' Sheila said despairingly. 'What d'you think's the matter with her?'

Jackie sat down on the bed, looking at me resolutely. She stared me in the eyes, and I was surprised that I had no trouble meeting her gaze. She was still beautiful to me, still warm and lovely. And I knew that she had my welfare at heart. I took her handkerchief, from under my pillow and gave it to her.

'Thank you,' she said, looking at it with puzzlement.

'What is it?' asked Sheila.

'My handkerchief. I wonder where she got it?'

She looked at me intently at the end of the sentence, or at least I thought so. I sank down on the pillows again, satisfied. But they looked at each other across the foot of my bed, and held hands. I shut my eyes then.

'What are we going to do?' said Jackie, putting her head on Sheila's shoulder. Sheila shook her head. I was quite amused, in a way, to be the focus of this much attention.

'Do you know how to contact her parents?' said Jackie.

'Well, not really. She must have an address book or something, but where?'

'No,' I felt like shouting. 'No, leave them out of it.' But I couldn't, I couldn't do anything, not even move again, and this was infuriating.

'She's crying,' said Sheila, moving away from my dressing-table, where she had started to scrabble about. They both came and held my hands, not realising that my tears were for my impotence, that they were intruding on my life and I was powerless to stop them. They would find out all my secrets and what could I do? Tears continued to trickle. I couldn't wipe them away.

The two of them had begun to turn my room upside down, taking the drawers apart, looking through my papers, my books, trying to find my handbag. They looked so desperate, it was rather funny in a way.

'Here,' said Sheila, sprawled out on the floor. She grabbed my handbag, which I used very little, and took out my diary.

'Diary,' she continued. It was just a slim one, with a few pages for names and addresses and a week to a page. The two of them sat on the edge of the bed. They poured over the diary, and gave each other piercing looks. I was trying to see what was giving them cause for such confusion. It was last week. I had written: Ray d, Pauline m, blood, what. I admit, I would have been puzzled about that in someone else's diary.

'This must be her mum's number,' Sheila said after a few minutes.

Just then, Eric came in. I could hear the noise of a man clomping about on the stairs, and knew that he'd want to come and see what was going on. Typical Eric, not liking to be left out of anything.

'Hello, Viv,' he said. 'All right?'

I tried to smile at him, and managed slightly. He looked quite alarmed.

'What the hell is it?' he said to the other two.

'Something's snapped with Viv, but we don't know what it is.'

The three of them looked down at me, like a bunch of doctors.

'She hasn't said anything to us,' Jackie said.

'No,' said Sheila. 'That's not exactly true. When I first came in here she whispered sorry to me when I moaned about the mess in the bathroom.'

The three of them exchanged puzzled looks, and I tried not to smile.

'Look,' said Eric. 'She's smiling!'

'What is it, Viv, for God's sake?' said Sheila.

I pursed my lips, and with the effort of trying not to laugh, because they looked so ridiculous, tears began once more to roll down my cheeks.

'Oh, no,' said Jackie, and she wiped the tears from my face with the pink handkerchief. They all looked a picture of tragedy.

'I'll go and ring her mum,' said Sheila.

The other two just looked at me. It was rather disconcerting, this constant attention. Suddenly I remembered what had frightened me in the first place. My face froze in front of them, I wasn't sure whether Jackie was on my side or not.

And Eric, looking so forlorn there, part of me thought I should be grateful for his love or whatever it was he was giving me. He was nice and kind and lacked a lot of the more risible male vices.

84

'Oh, Viv,' he said, sitting down. 'What are we going to do with you?'

My face didn't respond; neither did Jackie. They both stared at me, got up, moved around, sat down, stared at me again. Downstairs, I could hear Sheila talking to someone on the phone. Mum, I suppose it must have been. I could hear Sheila's voice rising and falling, and then the clang of the phone. Then she ran upstairs, faster than I had ever heard anyone run up them before.

She looked at me as though I had suddenly turned transparent; then, turning from Jackie to Eric, she said: 'I've just heard the most incredible story.'

Someone opened the door and turned on the light and I was in Yugoslavia again. I think Yugoslavia has always had particular importance in my fantasies because it's the only place abroad that I've been – apart from a day trip to France. This representation was pretty accurate.

I was walking along a coast road, the Aegean to my right, hills all around, covered in low trees, perhaps olives. And I was at the top of the hill, walking downwards, looking towards the flat part, and the next hill which I would shortly have to climb. It was utterly peaceful: no cars, no noise at all except for the clear sound of a goat-bell high up. The sea was completely clear and still, a golden sparkle around the horizon.

But it was the light which really made it special. And eerie. It was clear, the light of late afternoon, where the sun is still very much up, but has begun to reflect its light only on one side of the scene so that the bright side shines with strong colours, like a child's colouring book. It stands out too much, and as a result looks so much less possible than muted colours, toned down by the slight mist of midday.

I know that if I walk a little further, I will reach something

85

good and yet something frightening, too. I am quite alone in my walk, a solitary being along a solitary road – no houses, no boats, no signs of any moving thing except the goat-bell far away.

A few voices pierced the scene, but I could take little notice of them. The effect was similar to having the radio on when you're dreaming: somehow the words will tangle themselves up in the reverie.

'He died in mysterious circumstances.'

'How d'you mean?'

'Well, she wasn't specific.'

'I've never heard her mention him.'

'No, just a married sister. Nothing about him.'

As I walked towards the top of the next hill, I could hear the voices. I couldn't see their owners, but the voices seemed to be coming from all parts of the hillside, wafting upwards from the earth. This puzzled and disconcerted me, for I recognised their voices and, in some part of me which I wanted to hide for the moment, I knew who they were. Still, I couldn't see them, but coming up to meet me at the top of the hill were a number of other people whom I didn't know, not at all. I approached them with trepidation.

'Her mum was really worried, but not surprised.'

'Poor Viv.'

The sound echoed through my dreams, and the coming crowd seemed to echo it. It came with a humming: poor Viv, poor Viv. They swarmed towards me, coming, coming until I was surrounded by them, covered by the flow. So soothing.

'D'you think she's told anybody?'

'Who would she tell apart from us?'

They fell silent. They were right, it came to me in the dream, as the many unknown women, mostly blonde and with a few black women, but no brunettes like me and only one red-head, swept me along with them. I had a feeling that I knew them now.

The light was going, and the strange colours were becoming paler, now ghost-like. I could scarcely see in front and I dare not look behind. I wanted to fight my way out without hurting anybody, and knew that to be impossible, so I kept on going, caught up.

We entered a house, totally square, and many of the women disappeared. But about half a dozen stood with their backs to the wall, looking at me.

'Sit down, Viv, make yourself at home.'

I looked at her face closely, and it began to change from a formless thing to one of that woman. Or perhaps it was those women, I no longer knew.

'What is it?' I was tired of the lot of them.

'You should love this house, Viv.'

I looked around. There were strange pictures on the wall, and some photographs of little girls. The pictures didn't represent anything I could make out.

'How the hell do I do that?' I said to the woman: a very young one, younger than me.

'Accept it,' she said.

'No, I don't think we should leave her alone. One of us should stay here all the time until her mum comes.'

'What about her dad?'

'Let's hope her mum will talk to him. I don't think she saw him very often.'

'It's odd, isn't it, that although she talked quite a bit we knew so little about her?'

'But what did she say?'

Yes, indeed, what was it, I thought, drifting back into consciousness. I was leaving the women of my dream behind. I had had enough of the strange house.

Jackie seems to have been left on first watch, sitting on the hard chair. Funny to think I hardly know her, but she has been absorbed into our household because she is Sheila's lover. She isn't looking at me, not really, she's gazing wistfully at some point at the wall. I wonder what she makes of me. I seem to be inordinately interested in her appearance, fascinated as she twists her hair between her fingers. Black hair is so different from white. Yet appearance does have some bearing on the person inside: I'm frightened of her, yet reassured and desirous of her, too.

A hubbub, a flurry of people coming up the stairs roused Jackie. She raised her eyebrows at me, came over to the bed and sat on it.

'Don't worry,' she said, 'Time passes.'

Her kiss burned into my cheek as she stood up and, as I knew would happen, there stood my bemused and fearful mother.

Harriet looked at her daughter with sorrow and easy belief, even fulfilled expectation. She tried to banish the feeling that Viv was acting like this because she had had designs on Ray. Impossible. But surely . . . there was as yet no real reason to mourn Pauline. Harriet pitied Viv, true, but she did not understand her. It was more an empathy: a knowledge of their similarities even though she often could not see them. And they were so often irritated with each other.

'How often has she been like this?'

Sheila looked puzzled. 'Never that I know of, Mrs Foster.'

Mrs Foster! Harriet smiled to herself, and yet was hurt. Perhaps Sheila thought she was being respectful, but Harriet didn't want any kind of respect which she had not gained simply through qualities of her own making. And her slip made her embarrassed, too.

'I'm sorry, I didn't mean how often, but how long.'

'She was like this when we got home this evening.'

'Just lying here.'

'Yes,' continued Sheila. 'But I think she'd been out today, because I heard her first thing this morning.'

Eric made an impression on Harriet: she felt sorry for him. He seemed very ill-equipped to cope with this situation, whereas Sheila, whom she had met before, and Jackie, whom she had never heard of, seemed self-possessed.

'She has been acting oddly, though,' Eric said.

'Oddly,' Harriet echoed.

'Yes,' he said, rather snappishly. 'She's very distant, and says unrelated things, and tries to avoid us for days on end.'

Harriet stared at Viv, who seemed to be looking around the room, bored, but would not look into her mother's eyes. Pay attention! Harriet felt like shouting, it's you we're talking about, your future, your life. Viv's attention seemed to be flitting here and there, whereas worlds were passing through Harriet's thoughts. Like, I give you life and it comes to this; I give up so much to you, and both my daughters have let me down. But perhaps I have let them down, too. And John, well, he's let everyone down. Harriet felt like slapping Viv across the face. But instead, she said: 'Do you know if she's got a doctor here?'

They went once more in search of Viv's private life, into her papers. They were all puzzled by her diary, her address book. Entries were so cryptic, the shorthand she used almost unintelligible. 'Woman, why pillar?' Or, 'two days before: no way, no chance, no how.'

'What does this mean?' Eric asked. It was the passage where Viv had written Ray d, Pauline m, and so on. Harriet took it to the light, to see better what was written.

'Well, I suppose she must mean: Ray dead, Pauline missing. But quite what blood means, I don't know. There was a lot of blood, which she saw afterwards . . .'

Harriet suddenly wanted to vomit, but still managed to stagger to a chair and sit down.

'Are you OK?' she heard from somewhere far off. Then her head was shoved between her knees.

'Oh dear,' she said eventually. 'This is all a bit much.' She tried to wring out a smile and just about made it.

'Shall we call you a doctor?' Sheila asked.

Before Harriet had a chance to think about this, to wonder whether she really had the right to impose herself on Viv or whether Viv was seriously ill enough to be admitted to hospital, Viv sat bolt upright.

'No,' she whispered. And then, 'No, no, no, please.'

She finished on a loud note, practically shouting. They stared at her with alarm and horror. She stared back.

'Mum, what are you doing here?'

Harriet said nothing. She had seen her daughter in every appearance of madness, and now she was speaking just as though she had been having a good night's sleep.

'And you lot, what are you playing at? I've been asleep, haven't I?'

As she said this, Viv realised that something was up, and slowly the remembrance of it hit her.

'Oh, my God.'

Viv felt more alert, more in the present than she had for days. But things were no longer hunky-dory, and there was no way she could pretend they were.

'We were worried about you enough to call your mum, Viv.'

Sheila looked at Viv with exasperation, as though she had caught Viv out.

'Wasn't I asleep, wasn't I?'

Viv was full of horror, and began to screw up her sheet, mumbling into her T-shirt.

'Maybe you were,' said Eric.

Jackie, who until then had said little, got up and sighed.

'I think we should leave you two together.'

Eric and Sheila agreed so rapidly that they practically fled the room, leaving Harriet and Viv to stare each other in the face.

Seeing Viv crumpled small behind the covers, Harriet felt as though she was looking at her baby daughter once more. This child was terrified – and of herself, too. Neither of them had the remotest idea what was going on, Harriet thought. If Viv had been play acting, there would surely have been some sign of it, and of her wickedness for doing so. Harriet had noticed none in all the years she had spent bringing up the children.

Harriet wondered whether she should get into bed with Viv. Perhaps she was meant to sleep on the floor, or perhaps she wasn't meant to sleep at all. She was frightened, dear

God she was frightened, and the past twenty something years had meant nothing, had come to nothing with either of her daughters.

'Mummy, Mummy.'

Harriet was surprised to hear the small head from atop the duvet speak. And 'Mummy', too. It was years since she had last heard herself called that. 'Mummy' was rejected as an address when they were still at primary school, when bigger, more sophisticated girls called their mothers 'Mum', or nothing.

'Yes, I'm here.'

They seemed to have reverted to the positions of years ago, and Harriet felt her power as mother from that time. It was strong.

'Am I all right?'

'Oh, Viv, I . . .'

She tailed off. There was no point in simply saying she was, when she probably wasn't. Harriet's normal irritation when dealing with her daughters had by now completely vanished.

'I don't know.'

Viv sat bolt upright, stared at her mother.

'I thought things were great, that I was in control and I was so wrong. Nothing in my life is in my control. I don't even know how to get to work any more.'

'I expect you feel under strain because of all that's happened.'

'Yes, all of it.'

With this cryptic statement, Harriet did feel irritated once more.

'I think I've seen Pauline.'

'What?'

'I don't know whether it was her,' Viv continued thoughtfully. 'She comes and goes, you know.'

'No,' said Harriet. 'I certainly don't.'

'Once she came in here and sat on the bed. Another time I saw her on the tube. It was so real, but now I have my doubts.'

'What about?'

Harriet felt like getting up and pacing the room. This was sickness – both with Viv and inside her own stomach.

'So you don't know if you saw her or not.'

'No,' said Viv hesitantly. 'No, I don't.'

'Come on,' said Harriet moving towards the bed. 'Why don't you get back to sleep.'

Viv, to Harriet's surprise, snuggled down as though she was a toddler craving the security of her mother. It tore at Harriet's guts.

'You didn't tell them any of this . . .'

'No,' said Viv firmly. 'They would have blamed me, wouldn't they? Everybody would've.'

Harriet was unable to speak. She sat in an easy chair opposite Viv's bed, and began to stretch out. Perhaps she was right, that they would have blamed her, obliquely, because death is morally contagious.

'Just sleep,' she said eventually.

She was left to her own reveries, and they were not pretty. Guilt nagged somewhere in the recesses of her mind, although she wasn't sure about what she felt guilty. Then there was worry – about everything. She got up, walked around the room, and marvelled at the mess. Viv had been such a neat girl, but this was an odd mixture. In the parts of the room which it appeared Viv had not touched for a while, there was almost obsessive neatness. Tissues were creased together with knife-edges, boxes piled into each other, each pile at an exact distance from the next. But around the bed were heaps of clothes, many dirty, tapes, magazines and all sorts of clutter.

Harriet sat watching Viv, now asleep. It was very difficult to imagine what was going on in her head, rather as she had found it when her children were young. She had worried about them, worried a lot, but could not really have said how.

At the beginning of her marriage, she felt she was doing what was best. She had failed to improve her life before she was married, and couldn't see how she could improve it five or ten years later. But at fifteen years, it began to be different.

Meticulous planning, deciding when to go and how, that was it.

So when she met Marjorie on the course, and learned that she, too, wanted to abandon her past life, Harriet readily took off. By that point, both of her girls nearly grown and John completely lacking in interest in her, it was easy, simple.

Not that Harriet admitted any of this to anyone, except in part to Marjorie. To herself she admitted it one hundred per cent.

But looking at Viv there, she remembered the doubts. Then, they were commodities of which she had to rid herself. Now they were returning.

Quietly she eased herself off the chair, past Viv and down the stairs. In spite of it all, there was something about the room which she could describe as friendly. That was puzzling.

Downstairs, she found Eric slumped over the table. The room was only partly lit, and she thought what a romantic figure he looked sitting alone.

'How is she?'

Harriet shrugged: 'I really don't know. She's sleeping now.'

'And what are you going to do?'

I'd rather hoped you'd tell me, she thought, but instead said: 'Call a doctor tomorrow. She certainly needs more help than any of us can give her.'

'We've all been very worried about her.'

Immediately he said that, Eric regretted it.

'But she never told you why she might have been worried.'

'No. I thought maybe she would have told Sheila, because they used to be very close. But Viv's not close to anyone any more.'

'No.'

Harriet was too protective of Viv to allow the conversation to continue.

'Have you got a sleeping bag?' she said.

At *Woman's Day*, they made many excuses for Viv, but none of them was entirely satisfactory. For instance, if she was ill, surely someone would have rung in. On the other hand, such a conscientious and quiet worker as Viv surely wouldn't bunk off just because she felt like it.

'She's the sort of person to have secrets,' said Carly in the wine bar that night. They went there fairly often, but Viv always made her excuses. She didn't like wine, she said. They thought she was avoiding them: she could always have had fruit juice or coffee.

'Well, her flat-mate did ring and apologise.'

'Yes, Jean, but did you believe her?' Carly said.

'I believed her,' said Debbie defiantly. 'I don't care whether she has secrets or not.'

'She has been acting a bit strangely,' said Jean.

'But you don't really want to talk about it,' said Carly. She felt impatient. She was actually quite fond of Viv, but she really did want to get to the bottom of this. They sat and drunk their wine in silence, only disturbed by a band of men who pushed their little stools up close to them and were extremely loud.

'Well, no, I don't,' said Jean.

No doubt she felt her position of seniority. Anyway, she didn't like or approve of gossip, and she felt Viv's vulnerability. Once, she had been vulnerable and the target of many tongues herself. (Roger had been married before.)

Debbie, on the other hand, was not as vulnerable as she appeared. A loud shriek and then a scream hit them as a woman was pulled on top of one of the neighbouring men. Debbie winced, the woman's stiletto-clad foot waving in the air just inside her vision. She felt that she could understand Viv, although she was always exasperated by the way she put milk in her drinks when she told her time and again that she was trying to be vegan.

'Carly, we know nothing about her.'

She spoke with irritation, to which Carly responded in kind: 'Well, for that matter, we know nothing about each other.'

Debbie realised that they were aggravating each other, and

instead turned her mind to Viv. She was pretty strange, no doubt about that, but that was fine by Debbie. All this lot were too normal, really. They just weren't her cup of tea. Not that Viv was, but there was certainly more to her than Carly's fur coats.

A careering man broke into their meditations and, in one long swinging movement, sprayed a bottle of champagne over the three of them.

'You silly sod.'

I'm peeling away further and further: the layers keep peeling off. When I have finished, will there be a core of gold or simply the core of an apple, or the stone of an apricot? Things are coming to me that I don't want to hear.

There they were: all of them in the house, and mum, who I was quite surprised to see: inevitable, I suppose. But people have often watched me.

I was sixteen at the time – it was a couple of months after the wedding – and I was in bed with glandular fever.It didn't keep me bedridden all the time, but some of the time it wacked me. So I was asleep, but slowly beginning to stir, and I could hear voices. I opened my eyes, but slowly, so my flickering irises were barely discernible under my eyelids. I could see Ray and Pauline standing at the bottom of my bed, bending forwards as though they would soon topple over. He was running his tongue up and down her neck. She was saying faintly: 'Go on, Ray, go on.' He rather tentatively ran his hands over the front of her dress and she giggled.I felt humiliated to hear it, but on whose behalf, I wasn't sure. Her breathing came more quickly, panting now. 'Oh, Ray.'

Most of the time I had my eyes clamped shut. But I could feel what they were doing as well as if I was watching it, amazed at the highly-charged sex feelings they were emanating. How could she?

After a few moments I was compelled to open my eyes. It was very slight, but from the merest opening, I could see Ray staring me out, me, as though he wanted me and hated me all at once. I almost opened my eyes wide with the shock! Pauline was still moaning and groaning, and he had his hands broadly caressing her breasts. She was oblivious, and he, he was staring with his blue eyes quite transfixed. On me. It was a horrific feeling, and intrusive. Did he really think he was doing it to me?

I turned over in bed and groaned, leaving them enough time to adjust their clothing.

'How are you feeling?' said Pauline guiltily. Her face was still flushed.

'Oh,' I breathed. 'OK.'

I looked at Ray, wondering what was going through his mind. The obvious was just too disgusting. His eyes pierced mine: he had never looked so deeply into my eyes. And his glance now was one of acknowledgement, and of a smarminess which reaffirmed my suspicions.

'I'm sure you'll be up and about soon,' he said, and it sounded kindly. I could hardly believe that, because, apart from this latest little glimpse into Ray's inner world, he had never said anything kind to me or indeed anybody so far as I could remember. Certainly he had trouble treating Pauline civilly. But at this point he put his arm around her, and she leaned her head on his shoulder. Was this for my benefit?

'Excuse me,' I said rushing to the toilet, where I vomited up all I had eaten since the morning. This was what it was like to hate somebody; he had pushed his intimacy onto me. It was like rape, and I felt similarly violent towards him. Towards Pauline, simpering, newly-married Pauline, I felt nausea. But it wasn't her fault, just her stupidity to be mixed up with such a character.

Now, on several occasions past that first one where he had begged for forgiveness, Ray has been insinuating himself into my dreams, trying to persuade me that he's not as bad as I've painted him, that he doesn't deserve hatred, I can hear his plaintive little voice trying to tell me no. You've got me wrong. Anyway, Pauline has always been able to get me where she wanted.

Sorry, Ray, or rather not sorry. I don't believe you. I simply don't believe you.

Harriet hauled herself up off the floor, dishevelled from sleep, to see a dapper man she hardly recognised. John. She had deliberately not seen him for a long time. His wrinkles, existing then, were a little deeper. He looked down on her as one of his children, she thought – one who has not turned out as he wanted. How dare he? But Harriet was too tired to protest.

'What's going on, Harriet?'

His voice was quiet, reflective, when in the past he was never reflective. Perhaps, she thought, if she dug far back to their first meetings, he was reflective then. Indeed, that was one of his attractions. But that was a long time ago.

John, meanwhile, could hardly believe he had been married to the woman on the floor. She looked like an untidy heap, so pathetic. But no, he didn't want to be censorious. It was a hard time.

Harriet rolled over, pushed herself onto a chair.

'Hello.'

The two of them regarded each other as strangers – hostile ones.

'Where's Viv, what's happened to her?'

'She's asleep in her room, don't disturb her.'

John sat down opposite her, slumping, his neat suit – always neat now – looking rather rumpled. He had been up very early. They looked at each other, not wanting to see that the other had changed, even for the better.

'So that's what you're doing on the kitchen floor,' he said.

'They've had enough disturbance,' said Harriet testily.

It was hard for John when Viv was first born. Everyday when he got home from work, there would be one demanding child, one crying baby and Harriet. She was as likely as not crying too. These hardships draw you closer together, don't they? But John felt very sorry for Viv as a baby, not having the total attention they had been able to give Pauline.

97

'How did it come to this?' John burst out. 'Christ, when I look back on my life, what did I do wrong?'

He pushed his wispy hair back across his head.

'Don't you see that we all feel like this?' said Harriet. 'Why take it all on yourself? They are people, their lives are not totally bounded by ours. The four of us haven't been together for years. It wasn't your fault, John, don't you see? Nor mine either.'

I'm not directly blaming myself, he thought, but didn't say.

'So what shall we do?' she continued.

John stared hard at the ceiling, looking at the cracks, his eyes tracing their path. Water came to his eyes, and then trickled down his cheeks. But he was silent – perhaps Harriet hadn't noticed.

'We must call a doctor,' said Harriet stoically.

Something to do, she thought. Give him something to do so that I don't have to cope with all of this. There is so much to cope with anyway without the embarrassment of ex-husbands weeping all over the place. He lost my sympathy years ago.

'Do you have a number?' he said.

Harriet went quietly, pushing the door into Viv's room. How odd that he hadn't asked to see her straight away. The likelihood that he was afraid came to her – and went again.

Viv's uncurtained window let in a bright, white morning, glossy, glaring white, which almost rendered the sun unnecessary. Except that the sun would bring at least a little cheer. This just brought clarity. Viv was almost buried; her face was pressed into the pillow, and her body barely moved with breathing. Harriet reflected that Viv had changed so little since she was twelve or so, physically at least, whereas Pauline had changed profoundly during the same period. She became more frightened, and at the same time fatter, especially since her marriage. How little she had considered her, really, during the past few days, She might be dead or anything, murdered, a murderer, out of her mind with fear, when at least Viv was here in front of her.

'The doctor'll be round,' John whispered. He came in,

stared down at the lump of Viv. His eyes glazed over, took off and carried on out, out towards his daughter, with whom he had been on outwardly indifferent terms for so long. 'Both of them at once,' he whispered. And with him, too, the worries about Viv, about whom he could possibly do something, easily overtook his worries about Pauline, worries too awful to contemplate. The worries about both were there, though, with the sadness and the guilt that they should have known, thought, considered, And they had not. But then again . . .

'Trust Viv,' John thought aloud, and he watched the dead heap come to life. A quick stir and she had shot up.

'Trust Viv, what d'you mean, trust Viv? What have I done now? You're always going on like this, moan groan, never give me a chance to explain myself, never give me the benefit of the doubt. You would if I wasn't your daughter. Or maybe you don't give it to anybody. I don't know.'

That finished, Viv sunk back into herself, although not into the bed: she remained sitting. There was something three-dimensional about her: she was not of them, but had been superimposed.

'I'm sorry,' he said eventually. Apologies were new for him.

'Tsk,' she said. 'What's the point of apologising? You meant it.' She resumed her position in bed.

Harriet and John raised their eyebrows at each other. How bad was she? Her expression was vacant, as though she was awake and counting sheep jumping out of the window. Harriet could not tell whether she was just annoyed with them, or more than that.

'Viv, won't you say something?'

An expression of pain shot through her eyes. She shook her head. John was ashamed of himself, but still annoyed with her. It was typical: she always had to be contrary, even now. In some ways he had always been closer to Pauline.

Harriet was thinking merely about her children and how far away their births appeared. It was hard to imagine now that she had gone through all that, harder still to think of the years she had raised them to what? However true it was that the duty of parents was to let go, she had been fooled totally into giving up.

Viv, meanwhile, was not really paying them any attention. She had had one of those dreams which you cannot quite remember, but whose flavour is still in your mouth for a while, at least until you are properly awake. In bed, still in the warmth of half-sleep, you feel there is a body with you, something, someone warm and comforting. It was there until her father intruded. It was an ideal fantasy. And at the same time her guts were being pulled out through her throat. They pulsated, shrunk, and only then could she push them back inside. So she was whole, except that she wasn't: some bit didn't belong to her any more.

'He's in the hall, Harriet. I just let him in.'

There was noise outside: I could dimly see a crowd of people, and all the main players seemed to be there. I felt as though I was looking at a photograph in which the outlines were in focus but the rest, being so much darker than the area on which you have focused your camera, seems formless. You can just see a mass of shadows. Like criminals on television interviews.

'Let's have a look at her, shall we?' The doctor knelt down beside Viv on the bed, not seeming to expect a reply from her. She glared at him.

'Good morning,' she said. They all stood around, to Viv's astonishment. She said: 'Please could you leave. I'm not dead yet.'

They left, and the doctor began looking into her eyes, taking her pulse and blood pressure.

'And how are we feeling?'

'I don't know how you're feeling, couldn't say.'

'And you?'

She looked at him and shrugged her shoulders. 'Never felt better.'

'Well, that's obviously not true, is it?' he said gently.

'Look, how would you feel if your sister was missing and your brother-in-law was dead? Fucking brilliant, I suppose.'

'All right, I apologise.'

'Good.'

100

'But you know you've been worrying everyone by your behaviour?'

'Have I? Have I really?'

"Right.' The doctor, facing her, wrote something on a pad, but didn't give it to her. Instead, he went to the gathered crowd outside where they talked in whispers. Viv strained to hear them but could not. So she got out of bed, which was difficult because her entire stomach felt as though it had been reassembled very indelicately. She opened the door on the whole clan discussing her.

'Ah ha,' the doctor said, spotting her. 'Now then, young lady, I don't think there is really much wrong with you, but I've written you out a little prescription for some pills which your mother will organise,'

Viv glanced at her mother, who was ashen, and she inwardly laughed.

'Apart from that, I think that perhaps someone should see you who maybe could understand this – uh – situation better. I'll arrange an appointment. In the meantime, I suggest you get back into bed and someone will get you a little late breakfast.'

He was hustled downstairs by Eric, and Viv, standing mutely at the top of the stairs, was not sure whether it was herself she wanted to throw down them or a heavy object which would hit the doctor.

As it was, she remained timidly at the top of the stairs, head bowed, whispering rather than screaming, no. All this interference, however well-meaning. And as for getting her mother to look after her, what a joke! It might as well be the other way around. She ran back to bed, feeling her naked arms and legs very keenly beside the overdressedness of the others – particularly her father. What was he doing, turning up like this?

'What are you doing here now, oh *mein Papa*?' Viv lisped from her bed. It reminded her of childhood – he so large, standing looking down at her, while she was in bed. John was slim, upright, distant. And he didn't know how to cope with her.

'I was worried about you.'

101

'Well, I'm still alive.'

He could feel his anger mount along with his embarrassment. There was no doing this one a good turn. It was hard not to meet sarcasm with sarcasm: he would have to try.

'Did you get our postcard?'

'When was that?'

'Several months ago. We went to Madrid, remember?'

'No,' Viv sighed. 'I didn't get it.'

She stared at the ceiling for a while, and then transferred her gaze out of the window.

'Shall we talk about the weather?' she continued acidly.

But she was sorry, when he sat down, looking old and breakable. She had been cruel, yes, and that was all there was to it. She felt cruel, wanted to dispense what had been dispensed to her. Still, he had the air of dignified tragedy, he would not fly into a rage or break down. He would be forever dignified . . . in front of her.

'So Mum's got to look after me.'

'Well, I'm sure she'll do a good job.'

'I don't know about that. What about the people here, they could look after me.'

'I'm sure they've got things to do, jobs to go to.'

'I expect Mum thinks she's got those things, too.'

'Mothers always care though. And it's not as if she had to clock in or answer to anybody.'

'What about that woman she lives with? I suppose she doesn't count. Anyway, I can manage on my own.'

They remained silent for so long and John remained so still that Viv thought he must be taking root. She had thought him wonderful when she was a child and now they had no communication whatsoever.

'If I pricked you, would you bleed?' Viv suddenly asked.

John looked mildly surprised, that was all. 'I had a heart attack last year, don't you remember?'

'Oh, yes.'

And yet the inadequacy of their replies left a depression in the air.

Suddenly, John said: 'Have you ever seen Ray with a red-headed woman?'

102

'Don't know. I don't want to think about him.'.

'I see.' Of course, he didn't.

'I don't think I ever saw him apart from Pauline. Why?'

'Not sure yet.'

'There's not anything suspicious about Ray being seen with red-headed women, is there? Do you mean one person in particular or red-headed women in general?'

'One particular lady, of course, with whom I saw him a few months ago.'

'Ah . . . so you think he was having an affair, is that it, dear Daddy?'

'I've been dreaming about them since.'

'Dream, you have dreams and take notice of them! What is the world coming to? You're too earthbound for that.'

'In the normal course of events, no, I wouldn't take any notice. But things are not normal any more, are they?'

'Well, that's certainly true.'

Viv was remembering his intractibility in her childhood. When she was a teenager too, he seemed to be verging on a slippered middle age. But now, at least superficially, he had grown in dynamism and power of thought. Still, he pissed her off.

'And even if he was seeing a red-haired woman, what would that prove, if not what we already know about him – that he was a shit of the first order.'

John felt unable to cast the proverbial first stone.

'It doesn't necessarily even show that. I just need to know.'

'You just need to know, do you?'

Her voice was raised slightly: at moments, he felt it hard to imagine that Viv was meant to be ill. At others, he could see her disintegrating before his very eyes.

'Some things it's better not even to think about.' For I have thought about them, she reflected, and far too much.

Harriet pushed open the door, smiling at both John and Viv. She was carrying a tray.

'Here's your breakfast, Viv.'

Viv looked at it suspiciously. There was a cup, and what looked like a couple of bacon sandwiches.

'Did you just go and get that lot?' she asked. 'We hardly ever have stuff like bacon in this house.'

Harriet didn't react, and Viv, hungry as she was without knowing it, munched up the sandwiches and drank the tea.

'Good,' said Harriet, as she and John watched in satisfaction.

'Yes, it was very nice.'

Viv sank comfortably back into bed. It felt warm, and though it was starting to smell, she liked it. She sniffed away luxuriantly. It was like the fresh smell of a lover although, in this case, it was the fresh and stale smells of her own body. Her parents watched over and she had the curious sensation, not for the first time that day, of being a child again and having them watch her go to sleep. As she sank more deeply, as the figures of her parents receded into the background, as the whiteness of the sky took over, she had just time to whisper: 'You bastards, you've drugged me.'

Marjorie had seen Harriet off that morning with a hug and a flask of tea. Then she had gone for a walk in the forest. She felt totally useless: there ought, there must be some way in which she could use her powers, however slight they might be.

Her wellingtons sunk deep into the mud outside the back door. She would have laughed at the thought that their life was picturesque: to her, it seemed to border on the squalid, but it was theirs. She missed only slightly the comfort, the deep chairs, the fitted carpets, the space, in her marital home. It was not a bad marriage; there was just nothing good about it.

Now, if she could go deep, deep within herself, she could perhaps see something, visualise what had happened to Pauline. The trees: she stood and looked at them, tried to get with them into their greenery. How odd people had thought her in the past, she remembered, when she had told them about this. So she had to have confidence in herself, because even her ex-husband had had little confidence in her, except as the cleaner of the house and provider of meals. Neither of them was in the least interested in children.

Past this lot of trees, out into a clearing where the grass was a bit drier and she could smell the freshness. Like Harriet, she disliked the city. It was always the same, whereas the country was different. And it touched something in her. She belonged there. If she stood, if she stood and thought hard, hard, hard, then maybe, just maybe, she could get somewhere. By breathing deeply, by going into herself and at the same time being at one with the outside of her, that was the way.

She shut her eyes and breathed, hard and deeply.

Perhaps there was something, it was difficult to say. Images, people floating in front of her eyes, other images, other people.

Marjorie opened her eyes: it was all the same, of course, nothing and no one to alter the view. Yet she felt different, and so shut her eyes again. What was it now? Things in black and white were whizzing in front of her, as though she was travelling very fast through a tunnel. It was simply a vision of jazzy images, pen and ink drawings of something which she couldn't make out. She was curious; this had never happened before.

Then, flashing past her, came thoughts of Pauline, as though Pauline's thoughts were coming into her, were being tuned to her frequency. At the same time, more images were coming into her brain, but they were more solid, almost as though she was building them herself.

There was a small room, off a corridor, an old-fashioned corridor, with a hat stand and sickly-looking plants. It was dark, and she could feel herself propelled, or rather tripping quite lightly up the stairs towards a room which she could tell was Pauline's. The door opened, and there was a small bed with a candlewick bedspread, a small white basin with a gilt mirror over it, orange and pink wallpaper, and some gaudy, but dark and worn, full-length curtains. There was no evidence of personal habitation at all. The words 'I brought nothing' shocked Marjorie out of her contemplation. 'How could I?' the words continued. Marjorie realised that she was listening to Pauline, and Pauline was listening to her.

'Near Victoria,' this voice continued.

'Pauline is that you?' Marjorie projected very hard. There was no reply. What is it, please tell me, please tell me. But nothing. The strain was weaker, weaker, and ebbed away into nothing.

Before she lost it altogether, there was another image: of an old, but basically elegant house. It was white, with a sand-coloured front door. There were steps up to the front, and it had four storeys. This was it, she knew without any doubt. Pauline was here.

First there were hot hands, and moans. Then the flick of a tongue on her neck, and the sensations, the sensations up and down her back which she hadn't felt for a long time. The creepy-crawly feelings of dream love, dream sensation.

It was touching her – and it wasn't. That flat-palmed stroke of the hand up and down, it seemed ethereal; she could remember its touch, but never the actual point of feeling. Then the coldness, the shock of a cold hand, cold and bitter, then away.

And now her hair: it rustled her hair. Spread out on the pillow, what there was of it, each strand lovingly defined. Now hands again, now hot, on her face.

Her nipples stood alive, waiting, and while the moans seemed to come from all around, she could feel herself adding to them. But when she stretched her hands out to touch them, she could feel nothing.

Daring to open her eyes slightly, she could see nothing but darkness. No shadows, no clue, no flicker of life anywhere. Someone had taken the light away, all of it. But there was still the sound of noise, and the sound of breathing, and the wetness under her, pools of it.

It was delicious, this moment of unsurety, still with sexual trails alive around her. It was not welcome to have to face the world, see what was happening, and recoil. Where was she, in any case, and with whom?

Daring, she opened her eyes, opened them totally. She could see the brightness of the moon, round and full. Promising. This was the moon of romanticism, of love and of madness. It was drawing her and, she could see, it reflected the fact that she was quite, quite alone.

She was forced to realise that she was not part of this moaning. It was a strange awakening, for the sensations continued, and the sounds of sweet love-making continued too. It was hard to believe that her two senses, plus all the others, were combining to deceive her thus, that she was imagining it.

Now, quite awake, she realised that the sounds were coming from beneath her, from the partly lit window down half a storey and to the side. Sheila's room. Somehow they were involving her. They probably didn't realise it, probably would have been horrified. But their cries had pierced her sleep, had woken her. Deliberately, it made her feel alone.

And it was final. She was now totally awake and her body, although still alive, was sickened by the arousal. She had no part in this, it was theirs, their belonging. To each other. Their intimacy. It was the bitter taste of jealousy, fermenting inside her, stabbing her repeatedly, allowing her no comfort.

She looked at the clock: ten pm. Reaching far back into her memory, she discovered that she had been put to sleep about eleven thirty in the morning. So these drugs had worked pretty well. Out for all that time, and what good had it done her?

So: up and out she got. There was an emptiness inside her. It needed to be filled: how intensely she felt the desire for a lover, in all senses of the word. Clothes. And yet, at the same time, she wanted to be in charge of herself, and for no one to hold sway over her. But that independence could not conquer the gnawing feeling in her gut which demanded that someone do something about it *now*. The best way to conquer the feeling was to get up, to act, to do something. She dressed quickly.

Was someone checking up on her, keeping an eye? Probably. Quickly, she crossed to the window, opened it quietly and looked down. Too far to jump. Anyway, that was being rather melodramatic.

She shut the door quietly and, seeing the house dark except for the dim glow under Sheila's door, and the still-loud noises, she tiptoed down the stairs and through the front door. She was dying to have a piss after so long a sleep, but there was no safe way she could do it in the house. So she ran to the public toilet down the road, feeling so free as she did so. Lucky for her they always kept it open.

And now what? She felt like a runaway and realised, inwardly laughing, that was what she indeed was. Runaway from them and their painful passion, from her parents and their care and control. Control: that was what they were trying to exert over her all right. She would go up to London, get on the train, and, a Saturday night, there would be plenty to do, plenty going on. What she would do after that was anybody's guess, but she could not afford to think about it. She had to flee, to go, get away.

It was bright out, as she had thought, and rather mild. There was the first softness of summer in the air, and a strangeness about it. Perhaps that was the moon. She felt alone, but was satisfied in her isolation. She walked to the station, as though she was going to work, as though night was day. The trees were coming down to meet her, gathering her up. She skipped along, part of them, happy and anxious to please. Brightly she jumped, coming down again to feel the slight resistance of her baseball boots against the tarmac. Bound, up; bound, up. There again and again.

She bounced to a halt. Quick, doubled up in pain, hands on the pavement, unfriendly. Trees bearing down on her, something in her stomach, the pain about to quash the unwary. Crash! There it was again. What could she do about it? Nothing. Nothing, as it poked its way into her stomach, vicious, turning over and over remorselessly. And a feeling:

108

this pain is being wrung out of me, but I will feel it again, the torture of not knowing, of wonder, of fear, of a sensation that everyone in the world is unlike you.

Sitting on the pavement, again, even though she would rather have died than look face down at the gutter only months ago, feeling the knowledge of the entire universe out there, and her not a part. A dream fear made reality out of nothing. And not knowing, never knowing how or why.

A touch, a slight touch on the shoulder, and Viv was up, running as fast as her legs would carry her. Then, past the corner, she wondered if that had been an excuse to make her way back to the house: physical safety.

It was written on her shoulder in blood, that touch. She could feel it dribbling down her jacket, cold, slimy, sticky. Round the corner, she could not see who. But there was someone. And they were coming, they were coming, and she had to get back.

Running: and this time, the tarmac hurt her feet, vicious, but spurring her on through the discomfort. Could she hear footsteps behind? The pavement seemed to spur her on, too; it cast her upwards, propelling her like a pogo stick. Up she went; now down. Higher and higher. Through the door, breathing behind it, pressed against it. And relief, perhaps.

The house was quiet now, the love-makers had fallen asleep, or had at any rate stopped, because there were no more cries. It was silent, and felt very huge, bigger than it had ever done before, because it was not really a large house. There were just their three rooms, a bathroom and a large kitchen. But its reaches seemed to her vast and measureless. Where were they all, and where were her parents? She felt abandoned. They drugged her, left her to sleep, and then went. Cross: she was furious. But frightened still.

Up the stairs she tip-toed, regained her room silently, locked herself in. It was a pity there was no curtain, because even a tiny light might be noticed, and anyone looking really hard might see her even in the dark. She sat in the corner and looked outside. Gone the euphoria. Instead, she looked at the moon and wondered how ever she was going to get through the ever-extending future. Remembering, she touched her shoulder. But there was, of course, no blood.

Drawing her attention back nearer the house she began to realise that a shadow was now alive and coming at her, coming. Thirty seconds were too terror-filled for any thoughts. Then she began to see the shape of a fluffy brown head, and painfully gritted teeth. The eyes caught hers, and looked, pleading for solace. Her head seemed to rest on the window-sill, begging for admission. It looked severed. Or at any rate, it belonged to a body merely hanging on a thread. When the lips begun to mouth help at her, Viv thought maybe it was time to investigate.

'You cow, you stupid bloody cow.'

Viv looked at Pauline with all the exasperation she could muster.

'You scared me out of my wits. Was that what you wanted to do?'

'I had to come to you; you're my sister.'

'And what a touching little reunion scene this is.'

'I've been very stupid,' Pauline said sadly.

'Too right. So why are you here then?' said Viv starchily. Pauline mumbled, and Viv heard only the word 'blood'. Blood, she remembered, all that blood in a pool on the carpet. It stayed, this blood, stayed on her brain staring out into the centre of the room, until Pauline asked her what on earth was going on inside her head anyway?

'Blood.'

It was hard, they each reflected, to be in the same room as the other and not know what she was thinking. Their closeness came in flashes: this time, it was the two of them with a perspex wall between them. Not glass: this one could not be broken, and if you did anything to it, it would just become cloudy. But still, there was a thread between them.

It came in the form of messages for help to Viv, who was unable to do anything about them.

'Couldn't you have let us know where you were, or something?'

'No,' said Pauline sadly. 'It wasn't possible.'

'Why?'

She didn't answer. Viv looked at her, saw a rotund woman clutching her legs, recognisable as her sister – just. She felt enormous physical repulsion, without knowing why. That there was still a possibility that Pauline had killed Ray – for that she felt nausea. But maybe she hadn't.

Pauline smelt slightly, of a day or so spent rushing around, trying to get away.

'I've been in a bed and breakfast in Victoria,' she mumbled. 'I'm so tired, Viv. I can't tell you how tired. Tired of everything.'

'Yeah, I'm pretty tired of everything, too.'

The two shared a glance of mutual enmity.

'I can't forgive you for leaving us all like this, you know.'

Pauline grabbed Viv by the arm.

'Look, I'm sorry.' It was a grip which belied the sentiment. 'There was nothing else I could do. And I knew the police would come to you.'

Viv shook her off, and felt nausea once more. Perhaps it was true that Pauline . . . it didn't bear thinking about. Not even if Ray scarcely deserved the word 'swine'.

'I had to talk to you; I couldn't think of anyone else.'

'But we hardly talk at the best of times. We're not exactly a close family, any of us.'

'No, and perhaps that's one of the reasons why I wanted to talk to you. And you're my sister, we have all that past in common.'

'So we do,' said Viv archly.

'There's so much I want to explain to you.'

Don't bother, Viv thought. Then she grabbed Pauline's shoulders and shook hard.

'Why have all these people been following me, tormenting me?'

111

'What the hell are you talking about?' said Pauline, annoyed.

'Nobody I know's following you.'

'Somebody is.'

'Pah.' But she sounded less convinced.

'Help me, Viv, please.'

'What do you want me to do then?'

'Listen to me.'

'Don't I know it already?'

'How can you say that? When did you ever listen to what was really going on?'

'But we all know he was a pain and a half.'

'Just because you knew, doesn't mean it made any difference to me or even that you were really listening.'

'Maybe not, but there are more important things to be considered now, aren't there? Like you can't go on hiding from everything any longer. You have to work out what you're going to do.'

'So you're controlling me now, are you, coming on in the responsible sister way. Paying me back for bossing you about when we were little.'

'Oh, come on, Pauline, don't be ridiculous. Anyway, they all think I'm cracking up.'

Pauling laughed, pained and vicious. 'You,' she exclaimed. 'No chance.'

'What?'

'Look, stop trying to get all the attention for yourself, and listen to me for a change.'

'All right, OK, whatever you want,' said Viv wearily.

Pauline lay flat on her back, her knees bent up under her as in childbirth, and began.

'For me, the time between love and disillusion was gradual, and where in the beginning there was sweetness and love, so soon there was nausea and disappointment. We were both disappointed, we were apart. I went out of my way to apologise for him, make excuses like I always had. But there you are. In our daily life it was bitterness, resentment, with always the knowledge that in the beginning it was good, it was so good, it was what we wanted. It's the transformation:

112

they want you, they want you, they. The glorious Him, who will be adored for ever. A sweetness in your stomach which makes you, in one sweep, understand Romeo and Juliet, weddings, suicide pacts, and all the relentless songs on the radio. Except that it's all a lie. A lie, but I believed every word. I believed him, everything he said. But he didn't, not him. No chance. I thought I'd make something of him, making something of our lives, that we had to be together. But no. He just thought I was his wife, and that was that. To explain it, you have to see how I felt about him in the beginning, how much in love I was. I let Him take me over then, but that can never last forever.'

THE PAST

Do you remember when he first came to tea? You hated him on sight, glowered at him continually, practically spitting. Told me you didn't like his trousers; said his legs were too long. But I loved him – God! Even hated Mum and Dad for making him nervous. He used to sweat, said it was an ordeal. With Dad he had those awful men's conversations about work and sport, and he tried to tease Mum, make her laugh. She never did, of course, but that doesn't tell me much. I still don't know what she thought of him at the time.

She told me once that she'd never felt that way about anyone, and that she was relieved; that Ray soaked me up like a sponge, didn't allow anything to be left for me, and that for God's sake I was only fifteen.

But to go back to the first visit home . . .

'We'd like to go upstairs and play some records now, if that's all right.'

'Can you take the tea things out first?' said Harriet. She had picked up her knitting, not liking to have nothing – neither cigarette, nor tea, nor item of work – in her hands. The two of them moved, synchronised, towards the table.

They turned on a record, slow, romantic, because that was what Pauline wanted and after all it was her bedroom.

'Mm, Ray.'

Pauline had her arms around his neck and was nibbling at it. Gently – lips, no teeth. He had his arms slackly around her back, and was staring into mid-air.

'They liked you, Mum and Dad.'

'Oh, yeah?'

Pauline remained against Ray's neck. She wanted kissing, more and more and more kissing. Physical contact was what she had wanted all the time downstairs. Next to him: like this, not cold, inches apart, she felt alive and warm.

Her body was responding; his was indifferent.

'Ray, what is it?'

She had not been intending to whine, but that was what had emerged.

'Oh, nothing.'

He sighed, didn't move, kept his hands limp. She carried on nibbling at his shoulder.

Suddenly, he leapt into life and, pressing his mouth against her neck and shoulder, he began nuzzling and soon bared his teeth and bit.

'Ray!' Pauline was shocked: What are you doing?'

He laughed: it echoed round the room.

'I'm biting you and I'm going to do it again.'

He bit, this time harder. He took care not to let it show and as soon as he released his mouth, he edged it along and bit into another place.

'Stop it.'

She tried to move his head, and looked at him as though something strange had suddenly possessed him.

'Don't.'

'Just teasing,' he said.

Her tone was final but his, as he murmured then 'Oh, Ray, don't', was quavering and ridiculous. She looked at him with puzzlement and fear. He laughed all the more. The look in his eyes was conquering, vicious. His teeth ready, he sunk them once more into her shoulder, this time harder still. Her cries of protest dissolved into a choke as she began to weep.

'Stop it, Ray, stop it.' Her voice fed his guilt, redirected it.

'I'm sorry,' he said presently, as he moved his head.

She surreptitiously examined his eyes to see if tears were forming in the corners. They weren't.

'It's just that . . . I'm sorry. I'm a bastard.'

'No, you aren't, Ray. That's just not true.'

She cradled his head in her hands, covered him with kisses.

115

He took her hands off gently, and wriggled his way up from the floor. He stared down at her.

'Why do I do these things?'

'I don't know.'

He had not expected an answer. He continued to look hopelessly into space.

'I love you.'

'I don't deserve it.'

'I love you. And anyway, you do.'

They snuggled back down on the floor.

That happened for three years, all the time before we got married. It was so intense: he met me in the evenings, you already know that, and all weekend. After I started work he used to collect me from that, too. We were together far too much. But when we were apart it was because he wanted it, only ever then. He wanted to go out with his mates, and I accepted it. On the one night in my life that I arranged to go out with some of the girls from the salon, a forlorn little voice said, 'But I wanted to come round tonight,' as though he had a right to expect it. But when I wanted him to comfort me, he was no fucking good at all. I did everything, everything. Not that he seemed to realise it.

You see, I wasn't doing what he wanted, which was to change from myself into being what he wanted. All the time I thought: poor Ray, what he's doing to me is horrible, but he has such a hard time, and he's so screwed up, poor bloke. While I was thinking that, feeling sympathy, he was despising me more and more, you know.

Pauline put her hands up to her face, embarrassed but resigned to her tears.

After a couple of years:

'What's happened to you. You used to look really good in those trousers. What the hell have you been eating?'

'Pardon?' Pauline was defensive, but her attention was not entirely engaged as she cut up the chips. Ray stuck his fingers in her waistband, moved them around with difficulty, and began to laugh. It had a discomforting sound.

'You look like a biscuit barrel.'

Pauline carried on chopping.

'Did you have a hard day then?'

'You can't get out of it like that.' He laughed. 'How much weight have you put on?'

'I don't know,' she said crossly.

'Well, you look terrible.'

What's he doing, Pauline thought. I'm as disappointed as he is. Bastard. As if he looked that good himself. I hope he chokes on his dinner.

They ate pork chops, chips and peas, apple crumble. In silence.

'If you didn't eat so much, you wouldn't be so fat,' Ray began, the voice of sweet reason.

'Where have you got this tack from anyway? Nobody else has said that I'm fat.'

'They don't see you with your clothes off. And they probably wouldn't tell you anyway. Your friends are so polite.'

'Leave them out of this.'

'Look,' he said, sensitive to her misery. 'There are some really good diets you could go on. I'll help you.'

Do I look fat, Pauline wondered. Perhaps my clothes have got tight. I suppose I should weigh myself.

'And if you didn't drink any alcohol... That's very fattening.'

'I'd like to see you on this diet. No alcohol!'

'Yes, but I don't need to lose any weight.'

True. He looked as though he played many sports – a fallacy.

'Come here.' He patted his lap. 'If you lose some weight, I'll buy you some nice new clothes.'

They sat together for a time, she looking into mid-air.

117

'OK,' she said eventually. But her thoughts were quite different – of steadfastness and rebellion.

It wasn't long afterwards that that I left him. I took the day off work, packed up my stuff and left. There was a note waiting for him when he got home to tell him that I had gone and I wasn't coming back; that we were both making each other miserable, and there had to be an end to it.

I know now that if I was going, I should have gone completely. Disappeared. I didn't realise that at the time, didn't realise a lot of things, for that matter. Anyway, I went to stay with Maureen – you remember her – and she was very nice, said I could stay until I'd sorted things out a bit.

I stayed there one night, and went to work the next morning. I had half-expected him to be camping out on the doorstep, but he wasn't. He didn't ring me up either. It was about four when I got a phone call. He was in hospital, overdose. He'd taken a mixture of everything in the bathroom cabinet and then had rung for an ambulance. Still, he had taken so many pills that they only just saved him.

'I never knew that,' said Viv.

'No, we never told anyone. I wasn't sure whether he really meant it, but how could I have that on my conscience? Anyway, I was there when Ray woke up. He didn't notice me at first, but he looked around at the walls and ceiling like it was hell, like he had died and gone to hell, and water just trickled down his cheeks. I didn't know what to do. I couldn't move. But when I reached out and held his hand, he went into a convulsion – all stiff – and he snatched his hand back and put it over his face. Then he began to moan. I'll never forget those moans; the most horrific sound I've ever heard in my life.'

Pauline stopped and stared for a few moments.

'So what happened then?' said Viv.

'Just wait a minute,' said Pauline. Her voice was very faint.

'So after a while he stopped moaning, but he didn't say anything, he just stared straight at the ceiling with this expression of terror. I tried to talk to him, but he seemed to have forgotten I was there. The doctor told me to go home, that they'd keep him in at least overnight. When I got there . . . I don't think I'll ever get over it. I mean, the house, there wasn't one cup to drink out of, they were all smashed. He'd ripped the wallpaper off the walls, he'd set fire to the furniture – and apparently he'd burnt himself into the bargain – all the mirrors were smashed. He systematically destroyed everything. Everything. I had to go straight back to Maureen's.

'After that it was different, kind of. He was like a dog on a lead, a little lap dog, following me around, not saying anything. He abandoned his job, just never went back there, and anyway he was in no state to work. The hospital wanted to keep him in for observation, but he said he was all right, that we had our differences which we were working on. So they gave him some anti-depressants and that was that. He didn't really say anything about it, though. He just sat and sat, his eyes following me around the room. One thing he did say – the only thing he said to me on his first day home: "I'm nothing without you." And I thought, yes, that's true, I can't leave him, he'll do it again. So in some ways it was a relief when he started being snide again. I felt I could breathe.

'But, you know what, I'd never accepted, never, that we'd stay together. I always intended to leave him sometime. I mean, I've got a life to live too, haven't I? Haven't I?

THE PRESENT

Ray was around in the background of this dream. A shadow: that was what he was, a shadow. And Pauline was in the background; a shadow, too. I thought: so we've drifted off to sleep then, and this is the result of our conversation. There were many other shadows, and as I looked around the room, dark as it was, with flashes of light here and there, I realised that I was the only one not in shadow, the only one three-dimensional and graspable. They were will o' the wisps: as I put my fingers out, they slipped through. My parents were there, too, as was every other character in this pathetic fiasco, and some who are not. I was trying to get them, but nothing. I couldn't get them anywhere.

Suddenly I noticed that they were around me, all around. They formed a circle, all holding hands together. Oh, Viv, oh, Viv, they were crooning as they moved in on me. We want to take care of you, don't worry, you'll be all right. But they were shadows, and how could shadows take care of anyone? I could see through them, literally, their dark greyness like smoke. And the smoke would choke, would suffocate me. No, no, I tossed and turned. You must get away, you must. But they didn't.

I came back to consciousness quickly, into a day of bright sunshine. The first thing I noticed was that Pauline had vanished.

Nine am, and she had missed almost a whole day after taking those pills. Pauline had gone. And her parents had betrayed her, had stuck this stuff down her throat, which had done no good. Where were they now? It was outrageous that someone could do this, could believe they were doing the best for her.

Viv felt she would explode. Her chest was swelling, but her anger had no escape there. Instead it seeped out through her eyes with burning, burning tears. She was so impotent, no power, could not do anything, anything at all.

Her legs were still weak, the bastards. And why didn't she want to go to the loo? Surely she should? Her mind was already gone, and now they were sending her body to accompany it.

'Why don't you go to hell, Pauline. Go and join Ray, you cow!' Her words echoed around the room, sprang from side to side, ping pong, ping pong. She could see them, the letters bouncing with the force of coiled up wire.

She stood up, and accidentally caught sight of herself in the mirror. Her appearance was a fright. A tatty, dirty girl, with traces of blood between her thighs. She knelt in front of the mirror and examined herself minutely. Although she felt covered in dirt, there was no physical sign of it. Perhaps it was just sweat.

Her hair was plastered to her head like a wet cap. She even examined her knees, but there was no clue to be found there.

Eventually she looked at her face, closely, straight into the eyes. There was no more looking away: she had to peer into herself.

Her eyes frightened her: they were wild, and at the same time sleepy. She could see her anger reflected in them. It was the eyes themselves that frightened her and, more than that, it was she herself, a self who was also someone else, unrecognisable, who had to be acknowledged. She glimpsed into her own eyes, looked away, and then back. Her gaze had to be steady. So she stared into her eyes, stared until she felt hypnotised. Back in the recesses of her mind, she recalled that once the mirror, or rather another one, a distorting one, had helped her, had made her see more clearly, not evasively.

She took one last look at herself, and grabbed a hairbrush from the dressing-table. She tapped the mirror with the brush, then hit it hard. Harder and harder and harder but still, it didn't break. It wouldn't break.

She ran into the bathroom, and turned on the bath. She could hit out at the water. It wouldn't hit back but would simply make a noise. She shouted, too, felt great amongst all that warmth. She felt vicious; God, she felt vicious.

Suddenly, there was a bounding up the stairs, and a furious knocking on the door. It was Eric, back from a trip for the milk and paper.

'Viv, Viv, what's going on?'

She leaped out of the bath and opened the door.

'Eric.' She flung the door open wide, hair and body dripping. Eric stood frozen. But Viv was decided, overcome by impulse. She stood on tiptoe and flung her arms around Eric's neck. And then she kissed him, or tried to, at any rate. After ten seconds or so he took Viv's wrists in his hands, and disentangled her, pushing her away.

'Don't do this, Viv.'

'Sorry,' she said, looking at her feet. Suddenly she felt very cold, and dived back into the bath.

'I'll come and talk to you when you've got dressed.'

Her impulse had left Viv feeling humiliated. She felt more anguish about the fact that she had done it, than that he had refused her. How could she, how could she have done that? And what would Eric think? Who would he tell?

She submerged herself totally in the bath: head under water, she thought maybe this was how she would stay. But then it came, the panic, and she had to lift her head from the water, had to breathe again. Instinct.

Tears coursed down her cheeks, along well-furrowed routes. This was the bottom. She could go no lower. Viv sobbed for what seemed to be hours, wondering what Eric was thinking.

Eric was in fact on first watch, and was sitting in the kitchen absolutely terrifed. Was Viv's behaviour his fault? Of course, he reflected, she must have seen that he was interested in her. But the frenzied way in which she had attacked him was frightening. What were her real feelings for him? Hate, perhaps. He wished she had been taken into hospital.

Eventually, Eric tip-toed gently up the stairs, and stood at the door of Viv's room. He could hear nothing, and was very hesitant to, but he did so anyway. No answer. Surely he should go in, just in case – of whatever. He opened the door a fraction and could see, as he whispered the word 'Viv', a damp head pressed into a pillow. She was asleep, he thought, but wasn't sure. He felt sick for the mistiming of her pass. And sick with pity for her, too, who seemed so far gone.

Viv knew he was standing there, was not asleep. She knew he was embarrassed, was pitying her, cursing her mistiming. But they both knew that, but for the mistiming, it would not have happened. Still, her sense of shame was too great, much too great, to allow Viv to recognise Eric. She wanted to cry for ever, to be alone to weep, and this was just what she intended to do.

'What are we going to do about her?'

'What are the police doing about it?'

Harriet and John were talking at each other. Neither of them could have been sure what the other had said. Each was alone, quite alone and without comfort. But they looked at each other, how they looked.

They were in the nearest place from the house to have coffee: a café with ancient but attractive ceramic tiles. John found it distasteful, which gave Harriet yet more cause for irritation.

'She clearly needs help,' John said.

'Clearly,' Harriet said in clipped tones.

'Have you ever talked to his parents?'

'I don't even know where they live.'

'But the police have spoken to them.'

123

'I – yes.' She was sure that they had.

'Viv needs to go into hospital now.'

'No, I think that would make her worse.'

Harriet lit a cigarette, and left it to smoulder on the ashtray. John had given up in '76, but the temptation was always there. Still even that amount of weakness he did not want to display in front of her. The smoke added dankness to the greasy air. It hung, like Pauline's spirit.

'Do you remember that Pauline wanted to join the navy, just before she met Ray? It was such a strange thing to want to do,' said Harriet.

'I don't see why.'

Silence.

'We should ring his parents, contact them somehow.'

'You can,' she said.

'You think they would blame Pauline.'

'I'm sure they would.'

'Do you?'

Harriet was absolutely sure that Pauline had not killed him, but it was an intuitive certainty, on which John would put no credibility.

'I'm sure she's innocent.'

'So am I,' he said.

'So you'll say that when they start accusing you of having a murderer for a daughter.'

'Of course.'

He looked resolute, and Harriet wondered whether she had misjudged him. She handed him some paper with a phone number on it. 'They were out when I called,' she said.

John left the café in search of a phone box. Harriet was frightened: perhaps her trust in Pauline was less than she thought. After all she scarcely knew her daughter these days. Either of her daughters, for that matter.

John looked sad as he came back in.

'They weren't there, but I spoke to his brother. He was very . . . cold. Said they wanted nothing to do with us.'

'So what did he say to you exactly?'

'He said, oh, we were wondering when we'd hear from you. Did we know where Pauline was, and when I said no, and how sorry I was, he said they'd be in touch and put the phone down.'

'Threatening?'

'Somewhat.'

Harriet had had enough: she wanted to be free of John, but wasn't sure what she'd do when he'd gone. Traipse the streets in case she saw Pauline? Go back to Viv's and watch over her daughter?

'I want to go and see the police,' John said.

'Good idea, you do that.'

John expected respect from the police, and no doubt he would get it, Harriet thought. She wouldn't. She ordered another coffee.

After a while, Viv got fed up with the semi-comatose state into which she seemed to have drifted. She would have felt energetic, but her arms and legs refused to move. Her head was very energetic, though. Her thoughts weren't directed anywhere, they just were. All racing around her head, stirring up trouble. They looked like arrows, quite thick, and they became more and more numerous as they shot from side to side. Viv had images of them flying around her room and hurting themselves on the walls and ceiling, hitting themselves as they careered into it. Bang there was one, and bang there another. She could almost see them, and enjoyed the game.

After a while she got bored, as they seemed to have become tired. They looked like bits of thick bias binding, stage arrows, maypole ribbons: nothing with substance. But her head was still ticking away, wanting something upon which to focus. It found it.

On her dressing-table she noticed some scissors, and remembered that she hadn't cut her toe nails for ages. They were long: she scratched them against the duvet cover. Sitting up in bed, she began to cut her toe nails and gathered the parings very close together. She was on the last nail, a little one, when her hand slipped and the scissors went into her foot. It hurt, certainly, but she looked at the toe thoughtfully as the blood began to ooze slowly, spreading out slightly under the torn skin. Rich, red blood, like Ray's.

She gathered up her cut nails and put them in the bin. Then she looked at the scissors again, and at her toe. There was a deadness in her heart: she hated it. The numbness, the feeling that she wasn't quite sure what she was going to do next. She hated it all.

So, there was a way out after all. She took the scissors in her hand, which was strong and steady. Viv lay the blade against her arm, but didn't slash herself. She kept it there, feeling the coldness of the small blade. Nothing happened, of course, she just looked at it.

Then: enough, she thought. She hacked mercilessly into her arm, both digging and drawing the blade across. It went in neat lines: criss cross, criss cross. It didn't hurt, at least not to start with, but as she went along the first cuts began to hurt.

Now: she stabbed, now all her hate and anger spilled out against her arm, her soft flesh the martyr to her pain, hate and anger. Her whole life was taking revenge against that arm, that poor flesh now being reduced to mere flesh, pulp, bone.

That, that was against him; and that was for her father, and that her mother, and that her impotence, her frustration. And that, for Christ's sake, that was Ray. He could not hurt her, she would do it herself. She would hit, and hit, and hit, and then they would be all, all of them, and all her demons, out of her body.

She bounced back against the bed, her strength leaving her. It was done.

She lay, and lay, and lay there, thoughtless. After a while, she pulled herself up, and looked around. The room was a mess of duvet fluff. She had slashed it to pieces: it could keep her warm no longer. So what was this now, yet another illusion?

Tears began to rise up in her eyes, and then to fall methodically down her cheeks. Sobbing began, heartbroken. She was crying for her duvet, for what had been done to it, for the fact that she had done it. She would not, could not have (even had she realised it) cried for what she, they, life, had done to her.

Harriet walked very slowly back to Viv's. She looked at the pavement: back in Wiltshire, the pavements were generally level and weren't, as here, full of potholes and broken stones. The budding trees intensified her distaste for London. God, the smell.

As Harriet opened the front door, she stepped straight into Sheila, who was holding the phone. They looked at each other in surprise and their eyes locked for a few moments. Sheila put the phone down.

'How's she been?' Harriet asked.

Sheila didn't know what to say.

'Eric said she was a bit upset earlier. I think she's been asleep since.'

'I'll go and take a look at her.'

Harriet went once more up the stairs. Hearing someone coming, Viv quickly turned over the duvet. The other side looked quite normal, but if you felt it, there were considerable gaps in the filling. Harriet saw Viv's head, demure as usual, poking over the top.

'How're you feeling?' she said hesitantly.

'Just great,' Viv sighed.

She turned her head to one side, refusing to look at her mother. Harriet's thoughts began to wander: she could look around the room, think about John, wonder about Pauline.

'She came here last night, Mum.'

'Sorry, what was that, love?'

'I said Pauline came here last night.' Her voice was raised.

127

'How d'you mean?'

'She came into this room to see me, and we talked, and when I woke up she'd gone.'

The tears tightened in Harriet's throat, but she swallowed hard and breathed with concentration.

'Where had she been?'

'She wouldn't tell me, the cow.' Viv's voice wobbled. After a while, she said: 'I didn't believe it before, I thought she was a ghost. But she's not, and she's really tormenting me.'

'Oh dear, oh dear.'

The two sat for a while, silent.

'Don't you want to know what she said or anything?' Viv said loudly.

'What did she say to you then?'

'Nothing, nothing, just shut up.'

'Well, is she all right?'

John burst into the room.

'Ah, good,' he said, sitting down.

'I didn't notice you all beating a path to my door six months ago,' said Viv.

'Why, what happened six months ago?' asked John.

'Quite. Nothing happened.'

'Of course, we want to look after you when you can't cope.'

'When I can't cope,' Viv said with resignation.

John gritted his teeth.

'I was just telling Mum that I had a visit from Pauline last night.'

'What do you mean, she visited you?'

'She came into my house, as she had before, and then she went away without my noticing. I was asleep.'

'And nobody else noticed her come in?'

'Nope.'

'Are you sure?'

'Yep.'

John's arms and legs started to tremble. Viv stared at him, holding onto herself so she wouldn't shake, too.

'The police aren't ready for the inquest yet,' John said. 'They haven't gathered all the evidence.'

'But it's been days,' Harriet tutted.

'I'm sure they think Pauline did it,' John said.

'Well, I'm sure she didn't,' Harriet added tersely.

'If they think she did it, it's immaterial what anyone else thinks,' said Viv. 'When I've asked her, she won't give a straight answer.'

'What does she say when she's here?' asked Harriet.

'She talks about her life and stuff.'

'Come downstairs, John, and we'll have some tea. Do you want some Viv?'

'All right.'

It was so obvious that they wanted to talk about her, that she could hardly contain her laughter. She went to the banisters and leaned over, after they'd gone into the kitchen. But, hearing nothing, she went back to bed.

'You surely don't believe her?' Harriet said.

'Yes, I do.'

'Well, I think it's a delusion. You always did believe what you wanted.'

'Look.' He clasped her shoulders, their first physical contact for many years. 'I don't know about you, but I'm going to grab onto every straw I can, every one. I don't think Viv is that crazy: hysterical, weepy and nervous, but I don't think she's hallucinating, or communing with spirits. If Pauline is alive, under any circumstances, good. I don't believe she did kill Ray, but even if she did, we all know how he treated her. Just so long as she's alive . . .'

'OK,' said Harriet.

'Do you want some supper tonight?' said Sheila coming into the room, tentatively.

'I'll be eating at home, thanks,' said John. 'Maybe you'd like to come, Harriet.'

Harriet knew that she didn't want to go, that John expected her to, and that she would.

'Right,' she hissed.

'I'll have some tea now,' said a voice behind her. Viv had come downstairs.

'It's not ready yet.'

'I'll wait,' she said, sitting down. She crossed and

uncrossed her bare legs on the wooden kitchen chair, scraped at the edges. Her thighs stuck together and she tugged her T-shirt down, uncomfortable in the presence of Eric and her father.

'Will you be eating with us tonight, Viv?' said Eric hesitantly. He wasn't sure how much Viv was Viv, and how much a caged animal, on the point of going wild.

'I guess,' she said eventually.

There was a loud bang on the door; they all stiffened, and Viv sprang sharply off her chair.

'What the hell was that?' gasped John.

'The door,' said Viv.

None of them moved to answer it. The noise came again, in one crisp thud.

'I'll go,' said Eric.

Soon came a bright: 'Hi, is Viv there?'

It was Josh, and the sound of his voice made Viv burst out laughing.

'Ah, Josh, do come in and join the party.'

'Hello, Viv,' he said guardedly.

Viv felt strong: this was great! So all you had to do totally to intimidate everyone was to act crazy.

'How are you doing, Josh?'

She leered at him, and watched him shrink.

'Um, well, OK. I wondered if you'd like to come to the pictures, but I can see you're busy so I'll be on my way.'

'Oh, so soon?'

'Well, I can see you've got your parents here.'

'Oh, come now, don't tell me you're still in that adolescent phase where everyone treats parents like some beings from outer space.'

'No,' he laughed rather feebly. 'But I don't want to interrupt. I'll come back some time when you're on your own.'

'Bye-ee, then, bye-ee.'

She thrust him out, watching him almost run out of the door. But as he left, her attention was caught by someone going past on the other side of the road. A middle-aged man with white hair and a well-cut suit was walking disconsolately along. He didn't look at her, or acknowledge her in any way. But Viv felt that he was noticing her, and she had seen him before, although she didn't remember where.

A youngish man, running, caught up with him, draped his arm about the older man's shoulders in consolation. She remembered! Viv had first noticed them together at Charing Cross station. How could she ever have forgotten?

'For God's sake, come back inside,' said her mother. 'As well as catching cold, everyone will see you half naked.'

Viv allowed herself to be propelled into the kitchen. He can't have seen her, she thought, so perhaps there was still time enough. What was he after, was he an emissary from Ray?

She ran upstairs and flattened herself against the wall by Eric's window, the one from which you could see the street. True, the men had progressed far down the road, and were not looking at her at all, but that could be a ploy. No one came down their road by mistake: it was a silent, almost domesticated little street apart from the cars, as yet un-gentrified. The occupants of the street were either like them, or poor families, or people who had lived there for fifty years. It was inconceivable that those men should be looking for anyone of them: they seemed far too prosperous.

They were turning, they were turning back round and they were going to get her. God, it all stood to reason, and they wouldn't believe she had done nothing. Flattened hard against the wall, she dared to turn around and try to face them. She could hear their measured steps coming slowly up the road, not hurried: they knew she was there and, by God, they were gong to get her. Beneath their raincoats, she could see grey suits, again excellently cut, as far as she could be aware. They were dressed to kill, and no mistake.

Attack being the best form of defence, she would meet them head on. Heart pounding, she opened the window and shouted: 'Well, I'm here. What are you going to do about it?'

They stood stock still and turned, pivoting on the balls of their feet, to look. A wild-haired female was in view, half-hanging out of the window, waving at them, drawing atten-

131

tion to herself and, consequently, to them. They stood and stared.

'Come on then, I know you must be up to something.' She rested her arms against the window-sill. They turned to each other and spoke quietly.

'What are you doing in Eric's room, Viv?' came hesitantly from the bathroom.

'Nothing,' Viv countered.

Looking, more comfortably now, at the men, they turned to look at her. Shaking their heads, and with expressions of what looked like pity on their faces, they began to move off. After a short way, they turned back to look at Viv, still leaning out of the window. She felt triumphant, but it was muted: no doubt they'd return.

'I'm coming, I'm coming,' she shouted downstairs, as she shut the window and went into her own room to put on her dressing gown.

Ignoring her parents, she said, going into the kitchen: 'Two men are after me, Eric,'

'Are you sure?'

He didn't stop stirring the dinner, but he hit it a little harder. Harriet and John glanced at each other, and then away.

'Of course, I'm not surprised you don't believe me,' she said sadly. 'But it's true. Why do you think they're doing it?'

'Maybe they think you're somebody else, or that you've done something.'

'What? What do you mean?'

She barked so loudly at him that he splashed tomato purée on the wall.

'I don't know.'

'So don't say it then. Can't you see I'm frightened?'

Eric wished she'd go to bed, or something. Just get out, because she was making him nervous.

A door slammed, and there was a sound of someone running.

'Sit down, Viv, it's only Sheila coming downstairs.'

'No Jackie,' said Viv plaintively.

132

'Not every night, Viv,' said Sheila pleasantly. She went over to Viv and kissed her cheek.

'Are you OK?'

Viv replied by a welling of tears. ''Spose so.'

Sheila took her hand, and just sat next to her. Her parents sat, too, and Eric carried on cooking.

It's still dark, but it's not the same place as it was before. Help! Or is it help, I don't know. Am I inside myself or outside? The window has moved, the shape has changed. There is a little night light on in my head, in the room. Which is it? And when I get up to investigate, try to move to see what's what, I cannot. So what does that mean?

My eyes move, however, and my senses are still intact. I cannot feel anything touching them, and I wonder: am I paralysed because I feel nothing? I don't think so. And it comes to me that this is self-punishment. I am looking outside for blame, when I ought to be looking within.

Time passes and I watch it become light outside. I think of nothing: inside my head there is a huge blank, rather like staring at a pale grey wall. Pure white would hurt your eyes, but off-white merely stupefies them. And as it gets lighter and lighter, the dim realisation that something is wrong is confirmed. This is not my bedroom. It is not, is not, is not. But it's enough like it for me to wonder.

There's a clock alarm, which I can look at and realise it's four twelve; an uncurtained window, which is a little to the left of my window, and lacks a tree; a duvet with a different cover. It feels all wrong, and yet here I am. Now, how did that come about?

You see, coming about in the first place was unusual. I don't remember it, simply that before a certain time I have no memories. There are pictures of someone who could well

133

be me as a baby, but how can I truly be sure? It could be anyone.

Moving, little ticklish twinges in my fingers and toes. A tingling of life. Do I want that, would I not much rather be dead? Aliveness is a dangerous commodity, leads to pain, pain, pain.

So I could get up and I did, rising to my feet like one of those little foals, but with no proud mother looking on. She never looked on really, she was always in the background, acting some role or other. She was always on the lookout for herself.

But as for getting up and the reality of it: I couldn't be sure. I stamped my feet, trying to get some feeling back into them. Then I jumped, and jumped, like a school gym lesson. The fact that I had on a T-shirt and navy knickers helped. But as I jumped, higher and higher, I began to feel angry. Walking over to the windows, I started to examine the frames: they weren't mine. The paint was different: newer, not cracked. Out of the window, the view was certainly different: strange trees, strange cars. Certainly not my window. No, indeed: another street altogether. How odd.

The door was locked. Now my door has no lock, I don't think. No, I don't think it does. So someone (who?) has locked me into this strange room, wanting me to think, tricking me into thinking, mad and uncertain as I am, that I was still in my room. Now what would be the purpose of that? Either they want to frighten me or lull me into security. Two opposites.

I lay down and covered myself in the duvet. It could not be my room because the bed smelt of nothing, not of me, and the duvet was in one piece. I'd cut it up, hadn't I?

And then, covering many, many seconds, was the sound of the door unlocking. It clicked slowly, slowly, and as the door handle turned, I watched it with detached interest. Then the door banged open, and, standing on the threshold, was a woman with flaming red hair cascading over her shoulders. She slammed the door shut and sat down on the bed beside me.

134

'Viv,' she said taking my hands in hers. 'I've so longed to meet you.'

It was raining, drizzling and raining again: the sort of weather which Marjorie always associated with being in London for longer than a couple of hours. God knows how long this is going to take, she thought as she checked into a grubby bed and breakfast near Victoria station.

She lay down on her bed, with its mauve candlewick bedspread, and gazed at the pink checked wallpaper, trying to dispel the self-doubt. Relaxing, relaxing, she tried to draw thoughts into her mind. She pictured, as clearly as she could, the bedroom where she had visualised Pauline, and moved down the stairs to the front door. After staring at the door for a while, she tried to get her mind outside and into the road. It looked just like a road to her, with painted signs advertising 'Bed and Breakfast'. And there, hopefully, was a figure which had to be Pauline walking down it. This was not too easy, as all she'd ever seen of Pauline was a snapshot, one of those little booth headshots, which often bear not the least resemblance to reality. 'Pauline, I am here,' she said aloud. 'Please give me some indication of where you are.' But there was nothing, and Pauline remained remote, a pale, distant figure in a suit. Was it even Pauline, Marjorie wondered.

As she lay there, the energy slipping out from underneath her, staring at the uneven ceiling with a crack going diagonally across like a terrible scar, Marjorie wondered what else had happened in that room which would also leave scars. It was the type of room in which illicit liaisons took place, and she smilingly remembered how she had had one once, with her boss, and how, contrary to her expectations, it had been really nice, and she hadn't felt in any way dirty or regretful or in love. It had simply been nice. And now, somehow or other, it was years and years later, and she was trying to be psychic and trace a missing woman whom she'd never met, and who may well not want to be found in the first place.

She hauled herself off the bed and went to do something, anything. Victoria station she hated, but it was at least a point of reference. She walked past the police, the drunks, and the horribly normal tragics, and stood underneath Little Ben. She picked someone who looked as down to earth as possible.

'Excuse me,' she said. 'I'm looking for a cheap hotel.'

The woman had a kindly appearance, was the mother of three, and cooked for one of the nearby pubs. She could be my sister, the woman thought, as she took in Marjorie's fringed skirt and wellingtons. But Jesus saved me.

'Just down there and around the corner, and you should be lucky, love.'

'I hope so, thank you.'

'But beware of the crazy people around here.'

Marjorie just smiled, and said she would, thinking that no doubt she was one of those crazy people. When she turned the corner, she would be looking for Pauline, would be pestering people with her photograph, would be crazy.

Looking down the road, she thought hard. Was this road as she had imagined it, were any of these places as she had imagined them? Probably not.

After walking slowly for a little longer she decided, with a rush of resigned bravery, to bring out her photograph of Pauline. She tried it on the first person who walked past. 'Excuse me,' she began. 'No, thanks,' he said. The next person ignored her. The one after that, a teenage girl, examined the photo closely, deciding that she'd never seen her before, and what about the Salvation Army? That was about the ratio of response with the hotels, too: a few slammed doors, a few no answers, and a few very-helpful-but-nothing-to-do-with-me-love answers.

She went into the Wimpy on the corner by the station, put her chin on her hands and despondently stared at her coffee.

*

Harriet was most resentfully taking a bath. It was raining outside, and at home the rain would be seeping through the windows. Not here, though. The rain stayed outside; not that she could see it too clearly from her position, because the already frosted glass had gone steamy. They had never had such a bathroom when they were married, either. Couldn't afford it. But she supposed that both of them together in good jobs, with the money from John's parents' house too, meant that they could afford something quite swish. It made her sick. The towels were very comfortable, too: not damp, but deep and cosy. There was no way she could afford that sort of thing, nor would she ever.

Penny was looking uneasy but glamorous as Harriet, clothes on, went to see what she could have for breakfast.

'Hello, Harriet,' she said warily.

'Hello,' said Harriet, embarrassed.

'You can have eggs or something. There's bread in there, jam in there, and I'm sorry but I've got to go to work.'

Penny shot out of the door and re-emerged a few moments later.

'I'm sorry I'm in such a rush,' she said a little more graciously. 'I do hope everything goes well today. I'm sure it will.'

Harriet smiled back at her, but she was inwardly furious. The woman had the upper hand. If only there was a little more of that uncertainty, Harriet would have quickly warmed to her. She was married to John, after all, and for that she certainly deserved commiseration.

Following on from Penny, John came into the room. He, too, looked immaculate, and all Harriet's hard-won pride in her appearance, born out of a long period of not caring about it, was lost. He commanded respect as she did not, and it was more than the fact that he was a man and she was a woman.

He has weathered well, she thought, bloody well. But at least she had wonderful hair.

'Did you sleep well?' he said, sitting down.

'Very well, thank you.'

'Good.'

137

This was how it had been towards the end of their marriage, the two of them so distant that conversation was scarcely possible. Animosity there had been after the break-up, because both of them felt short changed by the other, but at the time it was just coldness.

They walked in silence to the police station, a squalid place, with a closed reinforced glass panel over the reception area.

'Sergeant Broughton, please.'

John was at his most officious, probably the best thing under the circumstances, Harriet thought. Still, she didn't like to see it. They sat on uncomfortable chairs, facing this youngish man with unchangeable features. Harriet was slumped in her chair, arms wound about her, whereas John sat forward rather aggressively. The policeman spread his papers neatly out on the table.

'Well, now, as you know the inquest has been adjourned until the twenty-eighth so that more evidence can be gathered.'

'From this end, it seems that no advance whatsoever has been made.'

'I can assure you, sir, that is not the case. We're both looking for your son-in-law's killer, providing of course there was one, and for your daughter, whatever has happened to her.'

'But we need more than that, man, we're just sitting around waiting, and nothing is happening at all.'

'I can assure you, sir, that is not true. Not at all. We're making every investigation, following every lead. For instance, the post-mortem indicated the possibility of either murder or suicide.'

'But our daughter . . . could be dead.'

'I'm sorry to say that may be the case. But it also may not. Without actual evidence, I'm afraid there is no way to tell.'

'This is all so vague.'

'Well, sir, I'm afraid that is the pattern with investigations. We are following leads, as I said.'

'What? No, I suppose you can't tell me.'

'I'm afraid not, sir, no.'

'Is there anything you can tell us, then?' said Harriet.

'Well, madam, as you heard a few moments ago, it is quite possible that he killed himself. Quite possible.'

'Perhaps after murdering Pauline.'

'That cannot, of course, be ruled out, I'm sorry to say. Forensic tests continue to be carried out. The angle of the wound, as you know, could suggest either action.'

'It would,' said John bitterly.

'If there's any further information we can give you, please be assured that we'll call you.'

'We are assured of that, thank you,' said John drily.

Outside, in the rain, the two of them gingerly held each other's arms and openly wept.

She was so large and dramatic that I could not but be mesmerised by her as she grabbed my hands. Hers were large, with the long fingers of the artistic. Her touch was gentle, and she stared into my eyes as though she were trying to hypnotise me.

'Viv,' she breathed. 'Viv.'

I wondered what this was meant to imply. I did not know her, I was certain.

'Who are you?' I said with detachment.

'Marguerite.'

Typical, I thought. She couldn't be called Jane, the way she floated so elegantly.

'Marguerite what?'

'I've heard so much about you,' she said, squeezing my hands. Hers were very soft, as though she had been soaking them in hand lotion these many months.

'Marguerite what?'

'Marguerite Dumas.'

She smiled slightly, her mouth going down at the corners.

So I had heard of her; certainly, the name sounded familiar, but from where I couldn't imagine.

'So why have you heard so much about me?'

She looked slightly fazed for a moment.

'That was Ray. I think he was rather keen on you.'

Viv removed her hands, and bent backwards until she was lying on the floor.

'What is this anyway?' she said.

'He's gone, hasn't he?' said Marguerite, tossing back her hair, tipping her head with it so that tears didn't come spilling out of her eyes. 'And I don't know why.'

'Nor does anyone else,' said Viv timidly. She felt frightened: perhaps she had been brought there to be intimidated.

'Oh, but someone must,' said Marguerite.

'Perhaps only Ray,' said Viv. She was steadying her hands by a great act of will.

'I knew him well,' Marguerite continued, 'but only within certain parameters: we were so very different. But I do know how bitter he was about the fact that you hated him.'

'What?'

'Yes, he even cried about it once.'

Viv buried her head in her hands from exasperation.

'That's the first I've heard of it, and I don't know that I want to hear about it now, either.'

'Oh, but you must,' said Marguerite in an icy voice.

'So what then?' said Viv equally coldly.

'He was a terrible fool, a real idiot. He used to tease me, and laugh about himself, but it was sheer bravado. I got to know him when he was driving for my cousins, and at the beginning he was so deferential. But he messed our business up completely, the business I have with my cousins. And he messed me up too, but I don't think he meant to.'

Her voice tailed off, and she stared at her beautifully polished court shoes. Her linen trousers and her cotton knitted jumper were limp with sadness.

'We were involved, and that was an uphill struggle. It was a passionate relationship in all senses of the word. We used to fight a lot, but after I threatened him with a pair of scissors, he stopped messing me around.'

140

Marguerite looked wryly at Viv.

'But he ran off with our money. There was a suitcase with ten thousand in it, and he took it somewhere. Suddenly, he was dead. I read it in the papers. And so, we have to find it.'

Viv hugged herself very closely.

'I don't know anything about this,' she said.

'I never expected for a moment that you did,' said Marguerite. 'But I have to find out how he died and what happened to the money. Will you help me?'

Viv pursed her lips.

'No, first you have to tell me how I got here.'

'Ah-ha,' said Marguerite Dumas. She stood up, and elegantly toured the room, turning as though on a catwalk.

'Are you a model?' said Viv.

'Oh, that was something I did once, certainly. But not any more: it's too unsatisfying.'

'You brought me here,' Viv continued.

'Not I alone. There are others.'

'You're speaking in riddles.'

'Something you do too, I believe.'

'Who told you that? Ray?'

'According to him, you were very intelligent.'

'How very nice of him to say so.'

'I told you he had a high opinion of you,' she said bitterly.

'I thought you said he was keen on me. That's not the same thing at all. Presumably when he married Pauline he was keen on her, but he had a rock-bottom opinion of her. She was an ugly, stupid lump who could never do anything right in his eyes.'

'No, he never thought much of her. Nor mentioned her much either.'

'So why did he think a lot of me?'

'Because you were living your own life, I think.'

This was uproarious, and Viv laughed until she began to cry.

'The bastard. How dare he think anything of me.'

'So you're angry with him. Well, I'm angry with him, too. He took our money and we're going to get it back. But I

141

have lots of tender feelings, too.' She sat down hard on a chair.

'You look far too together to have any tender feelings towards Ray.'

'He would buy me flowers, we'd have long talks about our emotions, about what bothered us. He'd had a very tough life, you know.'

'Who hasn't?'

'That doesn't mean we shouldn't have compassion for him.'

'No, it doesn't. But I've got plenty of personal reasons to have no compassion on him, plenty of times when he treated me like shit, like his wife's sister who was a dirty little kid who could never amount to anything.'

'I think that was what he felt about himself.'

'Or when he treated Pauline badly, and beat her up.'

'He did that to me too, and I hit him back.'

'Oh, for Christ's sake, that doesn't make it any better. So you hit him back, big bloody deal. I have no compassion whatsoever on a shit like that.'

'I don't believe you.'

'Tough.'

'Would you excuse me?' said Marguerite Dumas.

'I suppose so,' said Viv. Marguerite simply stood up and got out. She didn't lock the door or anything, but curiously enough Viv felt no desire to move. She sat on the bed, leaning against the wall, and wondered how such a sensible-seeming woman could have any positive feeling towards Ray at all.

Presently Marguerite returned, accompanied by the two elegant men. They sat on chairs quite far away from Viv, and averted their eyes respectfully from Viv's body, glancing casually around the room.

'These men are my cousins and business associates, Viv,' said Marguerite.

'You were checking me out too, weren't you? Following me, watching where I was living, where I was going. How dare you?'

'Sorry for any inconvenience caused.'

142

The elder man had changed his raincoat and suit jacket for a smart jumper.

'We had to find out where you were living to question you. We didn't mean to frighten you.'

'The hell you didn't.'

'I apologise if that is what happened.'

'We were genuinely sad to hear about your brother-in-law. Genuinely sad. Nevertheless, he took our money and we want it back.'

'This is the first I've heard of it.'

'Yes, miss, I'm sure that's the case. But perhaps you can help us. Do you have keys to his house, for instance?'

'Good God, no. I never went there if I could avoid it.'

'And your sister, do you know if she is still alive and where she might be?'

'If only I did,' said Viv, surprised at her daring and never for a moment supposing that she would tell them that she was certain Pauline was still alive.

'We are sorry for having to bring you here, miss,' said the older man. He was coldly polite, which Viv particularly hated. They were very definitely not to be trusted, and she wanted out.

'What now?' she said.

'We will deliver you back as soon as we think you've helped us as much as you can,' said the younger man.

'I've already said there's nothing I can think of.'

'What did you think he did for a living?'

'He was a mechanic, wasn't he?'

'Not recently. He was our driver.'

They were silent, which bothered Viv.

'Evidently he wanted money a little more rapidly than he had received it in the past,' said the elder man.

'I can't help you on this, you know. I really can't.'

'That's for us to decide, isn't it?' said Marguerite.

'Why don't you ask the police for their help?'

The other three laughed politely.

'I don't think that would be a very good idea,' smiled Marguerite.

143

'Wouldn't the police have found any money when they searched the house?'

'Of course, that is a possibility, but we have reason to doubt it.'

'Or in the garden?'

'Perhaps.'

'Well, do you want me to go and search their house for you?'

'I think that would attract rather more attention that we are aiming for, miss. However, as you are considered to be, how shall we say, a little unbalanced at the moment, perhaps it could be considered.'

'Perhaps he hid it somewhere else, or perhaps somebody stole it?'

'Your sister, for example.'

'I don't know,' said Viv weakly, after she had thought for a while.

'However,' said the older man firmly. 'This is our money. It belongs to us.'

'I believe you,' said Viv.

'Good,' said the younger man. 'So when we need further assistance, we know where to come.'

'Yes,' said Viv, shrinking.

He leaned towards her.

Sheila was getting her things together for work, gathering up her diary, her tissues, her wet-ones for when the kids put their sticky hands all over her. She travelled from school to school helping infants with learning problems and assessing what best to do with them. Mostly, she enjoyed her work. It was important, and after all she had spent years learning how to do it.

She wasn't in the mood today, though. Her home life was getting too much for her. Viv was just impossible, and yet she did care for her. Sheila blamed Viv's parents for not taking her away with them, leaving her and Eric with the responsibility. She wanted to be with Jackie, to let whatever it was develop instead of having a crisis on her hands.

But there was more, too. She had noticed Viv's idolisation of Jackie, the way she looked at her with glassy-eyed disbelief, scared and longing. Why?

Sheila had not enjoyed her own past role in Viv's life: that of surrogate mother. In some ways, of course, she was jealous that she had been supplanted by Jackie. And she was angry, too: did Viv only do this with black women or would anybody do? Guilty reactions beset her. But, after all, she wasn't going to dismiss her own feelings just because Viv needed peace.

She liked being strong and not having to ask for anything – most of the time. It was great having someone who depended on you, asked your advice, but they would always grow up, or transfer their attentions. As Viv had. And it hurt.

What was it that Sheila needed? There was Jackie, but despite all appearances, Sheila was treading very carefully. This was a first for her: it was a long time since she had been with anybody, and that was how she had wanted it. But she really didn't have the faintest idea what she did want out of life. She was no better than Viv: a little more self-controlled, that was all.

Viv's parents were obviously a problem to her, she thought, and she considered her own parents. They were loving: too loving really, but allowed their children no messing about.

As for Viv's, they were never anywhere to be seen and then suddenly, swoop! Then, off they go again. Not exactly caring.

Caring was what she wanted from Jackie. She had to have someone who would really understand her, who had grown up with similar problems and similar anxieties, to whom she would not have to keep explaining and justifying herself.

It was the first time, she realised, that she had had a relationship like that: all the others had a quality of elusiveness about them. One bloke had suddenly upped and offed; another had apparently been leading another life she knew nothing about.

And there were other, more subtle, examples. Viv, for instance; she didn't let you know what it was she was doing, but it sure as hell was something. Here was the proof.

But now Sheila wanted to concentrate on herself. It wasn't really that easily done, as so many of her thoughts were usually for others.

Neither did she want to be lumped together with anyone, and she felt she was being lumped together with Jackie: as her lover, as a black woman, as someone who knew her better than anyone else. She didn't want to be lumped together with Viv: as a friend, or as a person not able to stand on her own. Sheila wanted her problems and her virtues to speak for themselves. They didn't yet. But they would. They had to.

There was a soft knock on the door, a softer 'Viv?' and then a slightly louder knock.

'It's not barricaded,' she said.

'I've brought you a cup of tea,' said Eric, standing well back.

'Thanks.' She struggled upwards, and grabbed the cup, wondering for a split second whether she could ask his advice about her night. Eric stayed near the door.

'It's all right, I'm not going to bother you,' she said.

He looked embarrassed, and tucked his shirt further inside his jeans.

'I'm not going to work today,' he said. 'Sheila's gone.'

'You're looking after me then.'

'If you want to put it like that.'

'Why, what do you think I'm going to do?'

146

'Nothing, probably. Which is why I thought maybe you'd like to go out somewhere.'

Viv felt assaulted with joy and terror. It was a nice day, the leaves were on the trees, etc., and she was going to go out. But then what might happen? A dim idea flitted through her mind that maybe Eric was involved with those people last night, but surely that was too fantastic. Wasn't it?

'I'm not sure.'

Eric let her ponder for a little, and said: 'I've got no plans as to where we could go; it could be anywhere you wanted.'

'Oh.'

So he had no plans for meeting anyone; but then again, they could be waititng around the corner, or he could nip into a phone box to tell them where to come and Viv would be powerless to stop him.

'You can't see any reason why not, can you?'

'No, I suppose not.'

'Come on then.'

He smiled pleasantly. What did he mean, what did he really mean? Only a real fool would purposely take out someone like her just to give them a good time.

She got in the bath and washed her hair, as though she was going on a date. Yet it was like a date with her father: he was in charge of her every minute and would stop her doing anything naughty. Still, the scrubbing made the smell of last night go away. She wanted well out of that situation. She didn't want to think about people who came to get her in the dark, and she wasn't going to either.

She put on clean jeans and a T-shirt which surprised her, because she hadn't done any washing for so long that she hadn't known she had any. Then she put into her handbag her purse, a comb, every key she could find – there were many – some cigarettes, as she hadn't smoked recently, and the nail scissors in case anyone attacked her. Then, lacing up her baseball boots, she bounced down the stairs.

'What about Kew Gardens?' she said.

'All right,' said Eric warily, now that the initial enthusiasm had worn off.

They walked along silently, Viv feeling as usual self-conscious beside someone so tall. She felt childlike, as she had from the time of his suggestion. They sat on the station platform, Viv scraping her heels, and kicking her legs back and forth under the bench. It was a long way to Kew, a hell of a long way. Also parks and gardens were strictly Eric's territory. Still, it had been her first and only thought. She had never been there, in fact, not being particularly taken with horticulture.

'Have you ever been there before, Eric?' she said, with surprise that she sounded so normal.

'No,' he said.

They boarded the train, and Viv sat on the edge of her seat. She was relieved that there was nobody about. But when they changed trains, the people began to crowd in again, and she held tightly onto Eric's arm. She scrutinised everyone passing her on the train. They were all normal: no potential kidnappers or miscreants amongst them. Just solid businessmen and women on a day from somewhere. But no men who looked suspicious, or women who might be models, or then again women who looked as though they might rescue her.

Eric, beside her, was watching her stare at other people, some of the time with hostility. What was it about Viv? Was what she was doing total madness? That was a joke too, wasn't it? She was mad, yet what he was doing was total madness.

'They seem to be all right,' she said to him in a whisper.

'I'm sure they are,' he said.

They walked over Kew Bridge and Viv decided she was in fairyland. The sun was filtering through the leaves, as yet undirtied by the city grime, and she felt happier than she had for a long time. Little birds fluttered by the million from the budding trees, and their very selves seemed to be formed from the leaves. Viv stopped completely to look at them; Eric stopped too, but he didn't understand why. He saw the same things Viv saw, but with no sense of wonder.

A few magnolias were out in Kew Gardens itself, and they walked past them to the tea hut.

'They're so beautiful,' Viv said. 'So delicate, so graceful, they look as though they ought to be made out of silk or paper or something. They look indestructible.'

'Well, I don't know about that, but they certainly are beautiful.'

'But they are destructible, aren't they? They'll fade and die and there will be others and so on. Nothing lasts, does it?'

Viv began to sniff, and Eric was thinking, Oh Christ, to himself.

Prepared, he handed Viv a tissue.

With their cups of tea, they looked towards the budding rhododendrons.

'What a beautiful, beautiful day,' said Viv tearfully.

'Many days are beautiful, Viv,' said Eric.

'What a bloody philosopher you are,' said Viv bitterly.

They walked down into a wilder part of the Gardens towards a lake. Viv, watching the sun on it, wondered what it would be like to walk into it, full of weeds and whatnot as it obviously was. She wanted to be like the bloke in *A Star is Born* who walks into the sea. Viv wanted to walk into the lake. But presumably it wasn't that easy, and as you got into it the lake would smell and make you sick and anyway every human instinct was to make you get out and live.

'Shall we go somewhere else, Viv?' asked Eric. There was no answer, as Viv contemplated the feel of the warm sun on her body. It was pleasant, all right, but that was all.

'Let's go and have a drink,' he said, and they got up.

They sat outside under umbrellas and Eric brought their two lagers out. It seemed to Viv that it had been ages since she had drunk anything but tea – not even coffee. It was so typical that she be given tea all the time. Everyone thought it was calming, but she felt drowned. This slightly bitter alcohol, on the other hand, was a shot of adrenalin.

'You can have a roll or a scotch egg or something.'

Viv turned with surprise to look at Eric. She searched his expression for meaning: there was none.

'Yeah, OK, a roll.'

Food was never particularly important, and now it was not at all. She was more interested in the flickering sunlight.

149

People flitted around the parameters of her vision, but she didn't focus on them precisely. They were like the trees, but less natural. People were so heavily constructed. But her thoughts were not that formulated; they weren't really there at all, and how restful that was.

To the left of her focus, right at the edges, were two men, immobile. Her hands on the edge of the white plastic table tightened; her fingers stuck through the holes. What were they doing there? What were *they* doing there? Maybe it was all down to Eric after all. She rushed towards them, kicking her chair backwards.

'What the hell are you doing, following me about? Get the hell out of it, go on.'

The two men remained still, a look of surprise on their faces. Her arms were stretched out, and as she reached them, they both turned around to see whether she was really attacking someone behind them. Distracted, they did not expect her to push them as hard as she did.

'Get out of here, go on, get out.'

They moved back with large strides.

'Go on, go!'

Eric came out of the pub, and hurriedly put their rolls on the table.

'Viv,' he said running towards her. 'What's going on?'

'It's those bloody men. They're following me around.'

'Now, come on, Viv,' he said gently, putting his arm around her.

'We'll lose our table if we don't get back soon.'

The two men looked hard at Viv, and wandered back towards the road. She stared at them. They hadn't reacted at all, hadn't spoken or even defended themselves. Was it really them? She felt foolish. But nobody seemed to have noticed the altercation; the few people around were still drinking and chatting. She bit into her cheese roll, felt the pickle on her tongue.

'Why did you do that, Viv?' said a tentative voice by her side.

She shrugged her shoulders, and tears trickled down into her mouth, stopped her eating.

'I thought they were after me. Some men have been, you know.'

'They weren't, were they?' he said gently.

'No. Probably not. At least, I don't think so.'

'And are we going back now?' she said as she finished her roll.

Eric saw Viv's hair, bedraggled, as though she'd nearly drowned and then had dried it in the air, salt and muck sticking it together. He retched.

'Yes, let's go,' he said, and stood up.

THE PAST

Pauline once threw a whole pot of spaghetti sauce at Ray,
and because Ray ducked and I was standing nearby, I
was covered in it. It was scalding hot, and little pieces of
mince and onion bore themselves into my flesh, indenting.
The marks stayed for weeks. The wall, too, had to be
repainted, but Ray was spared.

And the last but one time I went to see them, about a year
ago, maybe less, they were having a tremendous row. I could
hear the shouting and the occasional thump as I shut the
gate and walked up the path. Pauline was shouting at him:
'Tell me the truth,' and by the time I thought I had to ring
at the door, Ray had gone upstairs. 'He hit his head,' she
said matter of factly.

Scenes from a marriage. Or, better in French for some
reason: *Scènes d'un mariage*. Their marriage. Their
Godawful, painful, mess of a marriage, which in many ways
was no worse and no better than a million others.

In the early days, they seemed absolutely bonded: against
me, specifically, and against everyone else. They laughed at
me, together; at Mum and Dad, together. They took no
notice, but I hated it.

And at times they would swelter into a maze of old-
fashioned gaiety; for the benefit of others, his friends mostly.
He would sit in an armchair, while she perched on the arm,
giggling at whatever tripe he was spouting: Crystal Palace's
latest performance; how many pints someone had downed;
Pauline's silly antics.

Funny, Ray seemed to be an only child, although I knew
that he had a brother, had met him once, probably at their
wedding. But when he was apart from Pauline, Ray was
solitary, un-connected, acting as though nothing and nobody
mattered. When he hurt himself with a screwdriver, and had
to be taken to hospital bleeding in a fountain so that I was
surprised he didn't die, he said nothing. He looked quite
calm, as though nothing untoward was happening, nothing

152

that amounted to anything. I guess that was what he did think.

THE PRESENT

Marjorie woke up with a start of surprise. 'Oh,' she thought. 'Searching for Pauline, whatever next.' And immediately went back to sleep. She dreamed that she was wandering through the streets of Victoria. People appeared to be coming towards her, would get so close, and then stare and evade her grasp. She was wearing a smart raincoat and so were they. All of them. And as they stared into her eyes, they bent their bodies and shuffled to one side. Marjorie was confused: was this a dance, a show, or an old cop movie? She knew she had no hat, so it couldn't be the latter. Yet she felt her hair, long and smooth, and knew that she was Lauren Bacall.

The breakfast was the usual. It was not bad, but Marjorie knew that fried breakfasts left her with a nasty bloated feeling. There was no one else around when she went down the stairs; the place seemed deserted. She had heard that hotel rooms were hard to get, and tourists were packing London. Perhaps she had landed in a brothel, and breakfast wasn't needed. Or perhaps everyone had already left by nine am.

But just as she was finishing her toast, another woman arrived and sat down, rather far from her. She was physically similar to Marjorie: similar age, similar untended hairstyle, similar air of unease and confusion. When she caught sight of Marjorie staring at her, she buried her head in her cornflakes.

'Excuse me,' Marjorie said, taking a seat opposite the woman who was forced to look up.

'I'm sorry to bother you and all that,' the woman waved her right hand in response, and inadvertently brushed her hair with it, 'but have you been here a long time?'

'A few days,' she said. 'Why?'

'Well, I'm looking for someone. A young woman who's disappeared. I've got her picture in my handbag. Here. Do you recognise her?'

The woman took the picture and scrutinised it, then looked at Marjorie, and once more at the picture.

'No, I'm afraid not.'

'Well, thanks for your time.' She went to get up.

'Who is she, anyway?' the woman asked.

'Oh, um . . . She's the daughter of a friend of mine, and I think she's living or staying around here.'

'And you're trying to track her down with a photo? Don't the police or the Salvation Army want to know?'

'They're being too damned slow.'

Marjorie felt uneasy: she was admitting too much.

'Many people disappear,' said the woman strangely. She stared directly into Marjorie's eyes.

'Yes, they do,' Marjorie said levelly.

She smiled, and moved to get up. 'It's time for me to be getting off.'

Marjorie went up to her room which overlooked many other rooms, also with lace curtains. She lay down once more on the bed and tried to clear her thoughts. This time it was more difficult: visions of people in cream raincoats came into her head. They persisted in staring at her as though she was mad, to an even greater extent than in the dream.

Marjorie got off the bed quickly, making sure she was wearing no coat, just a jumper, and went to face the streets. The sun had come out, which was encouraging. She wondered briefly whether Harriet knew she was in London. Probably, she would not be too pleased.

Soon, she was on the streets again, approaching hostile people, but getting nowhere. She went into a pub. She got a martini and lemonade and sat in the corner, relieved to see that nobody was paying her any attention. Perhaps she should talk to the people here, she thought, but she would finish her drink first.

She was staring haplessly into space, thinking of nothing, when she caught sight of a woman in the corner. She, too, was sitting quietly with a small dark drink, like coke or something, and a couple of sandwiches. She looked tired, as though the blood had drained out of her.

Marjorie looked down at the photograph she was holding,

and at the woman. She looked distracted, but not harassed or guilty. And yet the hair was the same, and her build and posture looked about right. She hurriedly put the photo back in her bag: if it was Pauline, she didn't want her to rush out. She watched her crossing and uncrossing her legs, smoothing her hair and, for at least ten minutes, not moving or altering her gaze except when she took a sip of her drink.

At last, Marjorie could bear it no longer.

'Excuse me, I have to ask you, are you Pauline?'

The woman stood up abruptly, grabbing her bag.

'Pauline, who's she? Leave me alone.'

'Look, I don't want to hurt you. Quite the reverse, I want to help.'

'I don't know who you are. Please leave me alone. I don't know anything about Pauline.'

'Please.'

But with one last look at Marjorie, a shot of fear, disbelief and scorn, she ran out. She walked quickly at first, slamming the pub doors behind her and then, when Marjorie was outside too, she ran quickly. Marjorie ran after her as quickly as she could, but soon lost her to a taxi.

I am not very deeply asleep. The great blankness inside my brain is becoming a sea, a grey sea with mist floating up from it. There is a vague sense of threat. It is all silent, unspoken. Slowly, I notice the mist clearing. The sunshine and bright, winter blue of the sky is beginning to show through, and pretty soon there is no mist left at all. But the threat remains, and something tells me that it is the fact that there is nothing, simply the sea and the cold blue sky, that is the threat.

Next I turn my back on the sea, and I'm walking through some scrubland towards the mountain. There seems to be a definite path through the bushes. Suddenly, I reach a road,

and move very quickly, as though I had my own set of
wheels. Try as I might, I cannot get off this road, and I seem
to be going up and down the hills at breakneck speed, rather
like a roller coaster, when unexpectedly I am turfed off and
somersault into a heap at the edge of a wood.

The wood is green and sweet-smelling. I hold my hands
out and absorb its essences, but still I do not feel quite
comfortable. I come to a clearing, and soon I see that the
trees are not all trees but some of them are people. They
have their backs to me; I have no idea who they are. But on
further consideration, I see that all the trees are people. They
seem to be at a cocktail party, and are all holding small
bottles of lemonade. A woman turns around and offers me
one, which I take and drink. It tastes pleasant, but unusual,
not like any drink I have ever had before. And then I look
at her face. 'Surely you went to Highview Comprehensive?'
I said. She gazed at me caringly: 'I do believe you're right,'
she said. 'But that was a long time ago. There's been so
much water under the bridge since then.'

As she turns away, I can see that all the people are women.
Then I realise that I know them all: Mum, Jackie, Sheila,
Penny, my workmates, a lanky, untidy woman with a placard
around her neck saying 'Marjorie'. I don't know her yet, I
thought, but I soon will and that's why she's here. An
unknown part of my mother. I glanced over the tops of their
heads for Pauline, but she doesn't seem to be included.

I can feel the strength of their lives shining through. I don't
want it, don't know what to do with it, and I'm afraid that
if I take it, then I might have to return it in kind. At least,
I think, the blonde women from the house have gone.

They lay me down on the floor and begin to stroke me.
Soon, I can see the face of Marguerite Dumas floating near
to mine.

'Viv, my sweet.'

'You here too? Why are you here?'

'This is for you, Viv.'

'For me, why?'

'You have to learn to trust someone, Viv.'

Her voice was becoming dangerously sing-song.

'But not you, not you.'

I wanted to call out for my mother; I knew she was there, and I needed her, but when I tried to shout, no noise came. I tried again to call for someone, anyone, but I could make no sound.

What a pity, I thought, that they should all be there and I could say nothing to them. What a wasted opportunity.

As Viv woke up she was seized with intolerable sadness, which wracked her body with sobs. This is what I need, she thought, and this is what I must have.

Marjorie had been given Viv's address in case of emergency or sudden news. How she might acquire that news had always puzzled her, but there you are: she needed it now. Marjorie had no ideas how to get to Lewisham, but she bought an A–Z and looked up Viv's road. She felt proud of herself: she'd done something clever. She is not dead, we've found her, Marjorie thought, fighting away the doubts.

It was a bleak trip to Lewisham for Marjorie, although she wasn't on the train for long. She had grown up amongst similar architecture and hadn't liked it at all. But there was at least a warmth in the north. Here, there were just estates, grime and emptiness. She got out of the train onto another busy road. 'Damn this bloody place and everything about it,' she thought. 'How the hell did I get mixed up with it, anyway?' She had a coke in a café with Victorian tiles and grease hanging in the air. 'And now this is all I can afford,' she thought bitterly. It was the poverty she really disliked, she thought: brought back so many early memories. She traced her route on the A–Z.

Once off the main roads, the streets were quiet, just a few people standing talking or a couple fiddling here and there with a car. It looked so suburban and most of it so tatty.

There were a lot of cars, but they, too, were mostly tatty. Even the bright, smart ones were not new.

Viv's house had no car outside, but it was comparatively smart. It had a ramshackle air, but nevertheless had been recently repainted. The path was cracked, and the tree seemed to have taken over the front garden. Still, it was an attractive house and she looked at it for a few moments.

A tall, substantial and hirsute man answered the door.

'Yes?' he said doubtfully.

'Is Mrs Foster here? I'm a friend of hers.'

'She's out for the moment. But, um, who are you?'

Marjorie hesitated, wondering whether she was up to dealing with Viv. Curiosity, however, and the feeling that she had come miles got the better of her. 'I'm Marjorie, Marjorie Pearce. Mrs Foster's housemate.'

'Come into the kitchen,' he motioned. 'I'm Eric, by the way.'

Eric waited for Marjorie to explain her presence, but she didn't.

'Do you know where Harriet is, when she'll be back?'

'She didn't stay here last night; she stayed with Viv's dad, but I'm sure she'll be around today to see how Viv's shaping up.'

What an odd phrase, Marjorie thought.

'She's over here a lot then?'

'Well, only over the past couple of days.'

'Yes, yes,' said Marjorie. 'Viv's mother and I share a house, you know.'

'Oh, I see,' said Eric, while Marjorie swallowed her smile at the inevitability of his thoughts.

'So, we meet after all this time,' said Viv, opening the door. 'I was expecting you.'

'Hello,' said Marjorie, now openly smiling.

'In my dream you had a placard round your neck saying "Marjorie".'

'Well, you've probably seen my photo.'

'I thought you were meant to be psychic.'

'I believe I have a gift, yes.'

159

'Well, why can't it be that, then? Aren't I allowed to be psychic, too?'

'I'm sure you are. We all are. But perhaps you've also seen my photo.'

'Yes, perhaps I have,' said Viv, defeated.

After minutes of silence, of sizing up Marjorie and quite liking what she saw, Viv said: 'Pauline's been to me several times, you know.'

'Ah,' said Marjorie.

'But she always disappears. She comes at night, usually, and then rushes off or goes after I've gone to sleep.'

'Why do you suppose she does that?' said Marjorie intently.

'She doesn't want to be pinned down. Perhaps she thinks that if I got her into my clutches, I'd call the police, and she'd be arrested or something.'

'So what do you think, Viv?'

The word 'Viv' hung on the air, and Viv shrunk under the weight of it.

'About what?'

'About Pauline. Is she guilty?'

Viv started to shake, and could only look at her feet. They were rather ungainly, and the toe nails were uneven. Damn them, she thought. People never usually look at my feet. With her voice very steady (a great effort) she said: 'I can't imagine it somehow.'

'So what . . .'

But there was a knock and Eric went to open the door.

'It's your friend, Mum,' said Viv as soon as it opened.

'Hello, Harriet,' Marjorie said as she came into view. Harriet looked bewildered.

'Oh, hello.' Explanations must wait, she thought.

'This is John, Marjorie.' He loomed forward.

There was a second when the tension was vicious, and then they started laughing: hysterical, drain-like laughter.

'We visited the police today,' he said without waiting for a word from Marjorie. 'And they were extremely vague and unhelpful.'

'I've seen Pauline,' burst in Marjorie.

Harriet and John blinked wide-eyed.

'In a pub in Victoria. It had to be her. She looked so like the photo, and then when I saw Viv, there was no doubt, even though they don't look particularly alike.'

'Oh, Marjorie, Marjorie.'

Harriet put her face in her hands.

'I knew it was the right thing to do.'

'Obviously,' said John. 'So can we have the rest of the story?'

'Well, I had the feeling that she was somewhere in the Victoria area, so I went there, and made a few inquiries about her. But I actually spotted her when I was having a drink in a pub.'

'What did she look like? How was she?'

'Oh, Harriet, I don't know. I went up to her, and showed her the photo, asked her if she was Pauline, and she ran off. Said she didn't know what I was talking about.'

Catching John's look of distrust, Marjorie said: 'I'm certain it was her. Why would she have run away like that if it wasn't her? Another woman would have told me just to get lost, or would have asked the landlord to throw me out.'

'So what now?' said John.

'We go back to that pub, and try once more to find her.'

'But, Harriet, she may not want to be found,' said Marjorie.

'She *must* want to be found. We have to know for certain that she's all right and presumably the police have to be told she's still alive.'

'And also that she hasn't killed Ray.'

Viv's interjection stunned the atmosphere only momentarily.

'I'm going back there tonight,' said Harriet.

'Of course.'

'And what about me, I want to come too.'

'Maybe.'

'I do want to, Mum.'

'Well, you'd better put on a few more clothes first.'

'You don't think I'd go out looking like this, do you? I'm not quite that crazy.'

She went upstairs to get dressed.

'How's she been?' they whispered to Eric.

'Well, we went to Kew Gardens and she got a bit upset there. After we got back she went to her room and to sleep, so far as I can tell.'

'What a pity,' said Marjorie. 'Was she all right before . . . you know?'

'She was OK. She went to work and to the pub, but she was solitary. We were always trying to get through to her.'

'Ah-ha,' said Marjorie, seeing much.

'But she was reasonably contented, I think.'

'Well, who knows,' said John. 'We each have things we don't pass on to anyone else.'

'OK,' said Harriet, thinking enough of these platitudes.

'I take it we don't tell the police at this point that Pauline's been spotted,' said Marjorie.

'They wouldn't take it seriously,' said John.

'But surely we don't want them to be after her, because then she'll run even further away. I imagine it's the police she's afraid of.'

'Of course, I hate to bring this up, but someone did kill him, whether or not it was Pauline.'

There was a silence.

'But we have to look after her,' said John. 'The police can look after Ray's interests.

'What if she did kill him?' Eric reiterated.

Viv, who had come to the bottom of the stairs, turned round and went up again.

'Then sooner or later she must face the consequences,' said John. 'for if she did, and I think it impossible personally, then she must have been acting in self-defence. I cannot and will not believe that she just killed him. It wouldn't have been possible emotionally nor, from what I can gather, physiologically. She wouldn't have been strong enough to stab a man to death. He would have fought her off and there would have been signs of it in the room.'

'I'm sure she didn't,' said Marjorie.

'So am I,' said Harriet earnestly, thanking God Marjorie was there. How much were they just trying to convince

162

themselves, she wondered? But then again Eric had a cheek, really!

'I'm ready now,' said Viv.

She was standing very demurely at the entrance to the kitchen, in what looked like a sweet little summer dress. How frail and in need of protection she looks, they all thought.

Look at them! They misconstrue me all the time, see me as they want; poor little thing; poor, crazy little thing. What does the doctor say about her and can she stand the strain of it? Poor girl, this has sent her over the edge, we have to watch her, watch what we say to her and keep an eye on her to make sure she doesn't do anything silly.

What a laugh!

All the silliness is theirs. Of course, they have always underestimated me. They always underestimated Pauline, too, but perhaps with more justification, or is that too cruel? Certainly my contacts with her have never led me to expect anything much, but perhaps she could say the same about me.

But I am preternaturally strong, can do things they never would have suspected. It's all adding up to a pattern. Ray has gone now, and they don't seem to know what to do about it. I mean the police! Not even being able to work out whether or not he'd been killed. What ineptitude.

'Are you OK, Viv?' said her mother.

'Fine thanks.'

The party was a little worried about Viv's demeanour. She looked strange; her eyes were glinting which they felt to be unusual and threatening. She was staring out of the window, with a piercing look at passers-by.

'Viv.'

'Fine, thanks,' she said distractedly.

'Viv,' more firmly from her mother.

'Oh, fine, thanks.'

Then:

'Oh, what is it, anyway?'

'I just wondered if you were all right?'

'No more or less than half an hour ago.'

'Good.'

Everyone seemed to be going about their business as they usually did, and I wondered how this could be. Why did they not realise that momentous things were happening or that I was here, in this car? Other times I would have thought there was no reason why they should, but they were other times. Now: now was different. I began to wind down the window.

'Are you a bit hot? I can turn on the cold air if you like,' said John.

'No, I wanted to open the window.'

Once again, there was tension in the car.

'It's just that it makes it a bit noisy.'

'I guess you're right.'

I started to wind it up again, don't know why. It just seemed the right thing to do. A few seconds later I realised why I had suddenly changed my mind. Marguerite Dumas. She was hovering at the street corner, waiting for the lights at the pelican crossing to change. She was wearing a very elegant and Sloaney Liberty print dress and pale blue court shoes.

'Oh,' I shouted, and pushed my head onto Marjorie's lap.

'What is it, Viv? What's the matter?'

I could say nothing. So far, she hadn't noticed me, and there was no reason to suppose she would. The car stopped to let the pedestrians across. Mum and Dad turned around.

'Viv, what the hell's going on?'

I didn't move; my head stayed where it was.

'Viv . . .'

I could feel Marguerite Dumas looking at me, heading towards the car. Suddenly we moved off again, and I edged my head up towards the window to check whether she had caught sight of all that commotion.

She had turned her head towards the car, as I could see from the back window. She was staring straight at us, and our eyes met exactly as we turned the corner. And coming from the other corner, going straight towards her, was that blonde woman. Her. I hadn't thought about her for days, because so much had happened in between that she had been edged out. So they were in league, were they? Well, that figured; that figured too bloody well.

Their house was only just around the corner. I waited until Penny had opened the door, and then sprinted inside.

'Can I have a look out of an upstairs window?' I said.

'By all means,' she said in a puzzled voice.

I peeped out from behind their bedroom curtains and surveyed the street. Nothing yet. But for how long? I could hear all their voices downstairs, no doubt wondering what was to be done with me. I looked out again. Still nothing. Perhaps it would be all right as long as I stayed out of sight of the window. But then what about when they recognised the car?

'Dad,' I shouted downstairs. 'Can you put the car in the garage, please?'

'OK, OK', he said in a placatory voice. And as I watched him put away the car without spotting them in the street, I thought that I must have won this round, at any rate.

Sheila was surprised to find the house deserted. The kids had been real little buggers today and one poor unfortunate had pissed all over her. She had not been looking forward to the mess and confusion of life at home, but the fact that the place was deserted was both eerie and an anti-climax. It was like the *Mary Celeste*: the inhabitants of the house had disappeared without trace, yet the teapot was warm.

She picked up the phone to ring Jackie. It rang and rang

for a long time, after she was convinced there was no one there. Oh God, she thought. Out when I need her.

She remained on the stairs, next to the phone, for some minutes after she had replaced the receiver. Where the hell was everybody, anyway? It was pretty strange for Viv especially to be gone. Why hadn't someone left a note, anything, to tell her what was going on? And now Jackie wasn't even there. Sheila sighed and got up to make something to eat.

After a while, she was buttering a few slices of bread for herself, the doorbell rang. Through the door, she could see two tallish figures, and, automatically, she hooked on the door chain.

'Yes?' she said through the gap.

'Is Viv Foster there, please?'

Sheila was not alarmed, merely astonished. There was no reason for these men calling Viv that she could fathom. Their clothes and general demeanour spoke of money.

'No, I'm afraid she's out at the moment.'

'Do you know when she'll be back?'

The older of the two spoke with utmost courtesy which left Sheila more rather than less suspicious.

'No, I have no idea.'

'Well, would you please give her the message when she returns that Ray's friends are most anxious to see her again.'

He bowed at Sheila.

'I wish you goodbye.'

She shut the door hurriedly, wishing more than ever that she was not alone. Still looking at the door as she unfastened the chain, she willed someone else, anyone friendly, to pass through. Nobody came.

Suddenly, the sound of voices and laughter came towards the door. Two figures could be seen just outside, fiddling with the lock. Sheila couldn't make out what they were saying, but it seemed light-hearted and intimate. As the door opened towards her, she saw Eric and Jackie, looking surprised.

'Hello, Sheila?'

Jackie came towards her and kissed her full on the lips; Sheila felt faintly uncomfortable.

'Hi,' said Eric, who went past her into the kitchen and slammed a parcel onto the table.

'I rang you a while ago, but you weren't in.'

'I'd probably already left.'

'Probably.'

Jackie put her arms around Sheila.

'What's wrong with you then?'

'Oh, I had a rotten day, and then this place was deserted. It's a creepy place to come back to alone.'

'D'you think so? I've always liked it myself.'

'Anyway.' Sheila felt all right now. They went into the kitchen. 'What's happened to Viv then?'

'Oh, her parents came to get her earlier. They've gone to his place for a meal.'

'And how's she looking?'

'Oh, you know. The same really.'

'Two strange men came asking after her.'

Eric and Jackie opened their eyes wider.

'Oh yeah?' said Eric.

'They said they were friends of Ray's and would be glad to be in touch with her.'

'What do you think that means?' he continued.

'I really couldn't guess. It sounds very suspicious.'

'Yes, it does,' said Jackie.

'Can we tell her?' asked Sheila.

'No. I mean, she's frightened enough that people are after her anyway. Let's tell her parents.'

'But perhaps people are after her. She's never spoken about them before, has she?'

'I don't know, Jackie. She shouted out of the window after some men, but I don't know who they were. I suppose it could have been these two. And at Kew she said some men were following her.'

'Is she coming back tonight, Eric?' asked Sheila.

'I don't know; they didn't say.'

'Well, I think they should have. We have lives to live, after all.'

167

'You know, a friend of her mother's arrived and said she'd seen Pauline, but she ran away. Apparently this woman's clairvoyant and a vision had guided her.' They all paused for a moment.

'Well, perhaps there is something to be said for it.'

'Oh, Jackie, after all you've said about mysticism in the past.'

Jackie smiled.

'Well, look, I'm going out soon,' said Eric. 'So who's going to do the cooking?'

The women laughed.

'You.'

'No, I've done it far too often recently. I seem to be doing all the turns which ought to be Viv's.'

'I'll do it then,' said Jackie.

'No, while you're here you're a guest,' said Sheila.

Jackie looked rather put out.

'You can help me,' Sheila said.

'Right.' Eric went over to the other side of the room and put on the radio. He watched Sheila and Jackie cutting the vegetables and slinging them into a pan. There was an association between them which was pleasurable to watch but which he envied. He couldn't define what it was exactly, but he knew that looking made him uncomfortable. He hurriedly got up and went out.

'What the hell's wrong with him?' Jackie whispered.

'What's ever wrong with him. He's a funny guy.'

'You seem a bit tense.' Jackie put her arms around Sheila.

'Yeah.' Sheila nodded. 'This is all a bit much.'

'Ah, it'll get better. She'll be all right. This woman will come back. I'm sure of it.'

'You really mother me, you know,' Sheila said.

'Well, maybe I'll need you to mother me in future.'

'Oh, I don't know about that, Jackie. You really seem together, all in all. But me, I've always been mothering someone, and I've had enough of it. I want to be looked after for a change.'

'You look after Viv a lot, don't you?'

168

'I used to,' said Sheila wryly. 'I haven't recently, not since a while before this.'

'Well,' said Jackie as she took a stir at the pot, 'You'll have plenty of opportunity to do it again as she convalesces.'

'No, I've had enough.'

She came up behind Jackie and put her arms around her waist. Jackie's body was slim and hard, a contrast to her own.

'Is that right?'

Jackie turned round smiling. She put her arms around Sheila.

'Hm.' And they looked into each other's eyes before they began kissing.

Eric watched then for a few seconds, but had to turn away and grab onto the banister. He felt a little faint. After what seemed to be a decent interval, he pushed the door open and said: 'Is it ready yet?'

Penny was surprised at how much food Viv was putting away.

'I'm glad you like my cooking, Viv,' she said, as Viv helped herself to yet more potatoes. Viv smiled.

'I'm really hungry,' she said. 'I don't seem to be eating very much at the moment.'

The meal had been conducted with very little conversation. None of them knew what they could talk about: all usual topics of conversation were irrelevant; pertinent topics would be too upsetting. Viv had to be kept calm: the pills the doctor had prescribed made her sleep, but not sedate.

'And what sort of food do you like, Viv? Apparently you're vegetarian in your house.'

'Well, usually. But we eat fish and if we go to restaurants, which we do occasionally, we eat meat. None of us is a vegetarian out of conviction. I mean, I like roast dinners and

169

curries and the sort of stews we used to eat when I was little. I don't suppose Mum makes them now. I mean,' she popped a potato into her mouth. 'It's cheapness as much as anything. And I like ice-cream and fancy cheese and sausage rolls and bacon sandwiches.'

'I made you one the other day,' interjected Harriet.

'Yes, it was nice. But otherwise I haven't been fancying food very much.'

'Well, you're certainly making up for that now,' remarked her father.

'I should hope I am,' she smiled.

None of them knew what to make of this. But then they found it hard to know what to make of Viv these days.

'I mean, there are no drugs in this, are there?'

'We don't habitually drug your food. It was just the once.'

'Well, it was once too often.'

Viv put down her knife and fork.

'Do you think I've aged?' she said.

'Oh, for God's sake. You're only twenty-one.'

'That's twenty-one years older than being a baby.'

'Yes, and it's twenty-five years younger than me. Don't be ridiculous,' said John.

'I can see lines now where I've never seen them before. I just looked at my face before we had this meal. I'm looking hollow, empty, and my skin looks funny.'

'Well, to me, twenty-one is scarcely older than a baby,' said Harriet.

'What did you tell my job?' she continued to her mother through a mouthful of Brussels sprouts.

'That you were suffering a lot of strain and the doctor said you had to rest for a while. We sent them a sick note.'

'Thanks, Mum. Wonderful.'

She ate some more, then leaned back in her chair.

'Excellent cooking, Mrs Foster.'

The others all winced.

'Thanks, Viv.'

'Does Dad ever cook now?'

'I do it occasionally. I have improved slightly.'

'So I should hope.'

170

They began to clear the dishes from the table, and passed them to Penny.

'You know, two women spotted me as we turned into this road and I'm sure they're going to find out I'm here sooner or later.'

'Why's that then?' said Marjorie.

'Something to do with Ray running off with some money.'

'Oh, really.'

'One of them looks like Pauline but is a bit fatter and the other one's a really stunning woman with red hair who calls herself Marguerite Dumas.'

'Sounds French,' said Harriet.

'I've seen a woman who looks like that with Ray.'

'Of course!' Viv was now very interested. 'I remember you saying.'

'A few months ago. I was in the car, and they were coming out of a house, talking hard. I put it to the back of my mind, thought they should sort out their own affairs.'

John shifted about in a guilty way.

'I never liked Ray,' said Harriet.

'Well, that makes all of us.'

'Yes, Viv, but it seems rather unfeeling to say it when he's dead.'

'I'd say it was hypocritical not to.'

'In any case, Pauline wouldn't have been dissuaded from marrying him. If we'd stuck out against it, things would only have got a lot worse.'

'I should have said something. Maybe then she wouldn't have.'

'Oh, come on, Dad, don't be daft.'

Viv raised her eyes to the ceiling in exasperation.

'Anyway, they'll get me, those two women. I can't escape even here.'

'We'll look after you, don't worry,' Penny said calmly.

Harriet and John accidentally exchanged looks.

'Can I go to bed then?' asked Viv.

'But it's only nine,' protested Harriet.

'I want to go to bed,' said Viv firmly.

171

'That's OK,' said Penny. 'I'll go and make up a bed for you.'

She trotted elegantly up the stairs, her court shoes only slightly indenting the beige carpet. Viv watched her backside in the flowered dress spring from side to side. What energy, she thought. Perhaps Dad loved her energy. Mum had never had that energy; neither had she, for that matter. Everyone seemed old beside Penny, even she, who must be about fifteen years younger.

The remaining four of them were seated around the oval table. Viv rested her chin on her hand, the weight of her head pushing her hand towards the table. A quick survey of the others showed Harriet staring at the space where Penny had been; John examining a part of the ceiling he had missed when he painted it six months ago; and Marjorie twisting a ring round and around her finger. How loose it was, Viv thought. Had her finger shrunk? Why would anyone buy a ring that loose?

'The room's all ready, Viv,' Penny smiled. 'Shall we go up?'

Viv held her hand out wordlessly to her mother for her pill. Swallowing it, she shuddered, got up slowly, and pushed her chair to the table. She passed a pale smile around the table. How soft the carpet felt as she walked up the stairs, she thought. But her hands could touch the wall at either side of her with her elbows bent, she discovered as she went up the stairs. What an odd house, she thought. In some ways it was like a little doll's house with tiny corridors and some of the rooms like cupboards. Yet the main living room took up a whole floor, and seemed enormous.

'I hope you'll be comfortable, Viv,' said Penny as she opened the bedroom door. It was odd, Viv reflected, how Penny inspired warmth.

'You know where the bathroom is.'

She was gone.

As she shut the door, Viv scooted to the window and took up position near the curtain. It was just dark, and the sky was navy blue, but as far as she could see there were no suspicious characters in this pleasant, sloping, tree-lined street of town houses. After a while of intense surveillance, Viv opened the window and leaned out. It was a modern window: only one side of it opened and so leaning out was difficult, which Viv regretted. She still could not be absolutely certain that nobody was there. The air was not particularly warm, but it smelt so fresh. John and Penny lived not too far out in the suburbs, but for some reason it felt as though they were living in the middle of a forest. Trees: yews, pines, chestnuts, all there giving out whatever it is that trees give out. A sense of well-being, perhaps. Still, she could not hope to aspire to that.

Was that a movement under the tree over there? It was difficult to tell. Better to go to bed, to luxuriate in what appeared to be a comfortable, pomander-scented bed with a duvet whose softness surpassed anything she had previously enjoyed. Viv squashed it between her fingers and pressed it up against her cheek. She wanted to stay here, not to go back to her house ever again with its sparse, decaying furniture and perpetual battle against dirt, which they constantly abandoned. This was their spare bedroom and, even though it was tiny, it was decorated with thought and care and was cleaner than any room where she had stayed before. It must be something to do with the fact that the house was new. New. Viv was fed up with old, was fed up with so many things. But this room, with its general air of pale green comfort, could have been any similar room anywhere, or so she imagined, never having been in any similar room.

She opened the door to hear what they were saying. In fact, she could make out little, and tiptoed in bare feet down the stairs. The door to the living room was closed, but she could hear the rough outlines of a conversation. Oddly, she thought, it was about which television programme to watch. Why weren't they talking about Pauline? She noticed Marjorie's voice, too: she had said nothing since she had arrived. Viv's stomach pulled a little: there were more important things to be considering.

By now she was feeling a little sleepy, and knew that exactly what she needed was hot water. She ran it into the bath so hot that she was pink for the rest of the night. It

173

raised her body temperature. She had read somewhere that people who were dying of exposure could be brought back from certain death with a hot bath.

In bed, to the faint sound of gunfire coming from the room below, Viv fell asleep.

Her dreams were full of steep hills. They wouldn't quite have qualified as mountains; however, they seemed to go up and up. For some time, she was walking along a moor covered in pinkish heather. The whole vista, as far as the eye could see, was of a pinkish covering on dark green, the sky a whitish grey. It was totally quiet, so quiet that the silence roared. Viv walked and walked. She was not tired, but was aware that she had been walking for a long time, so long that she could not remember when it had started. Soon she became aware that she was going up. The moor had turned into a hill which became steeper and steeper. There was nothing for it but to push on.

As the hill became so steep that it was almost impossible to carry on for fear of sliding back down again, Viv discovered an opening in the side of the hill. She would have to stoop to get in, but there would be a resting place. Inside, she found she could stand up. It was dark, not totally dark, because the ghostly grey-white of the sky made a faint impression, but too dark to make out much. She felt the walls: they were a gooey, icy kind of smooth rock which had the texture of plastic. As she felt around the rock, going into the darker part of the cave, she noticed that it turned a corner. So did she, and saw a light far down the end of the tunnel. Feeling small rocks beneath her feet, she tramped down towards it. A shift of recognition took place within her. They were there: it was another cocktail party. All those women, those bloody women were there, forcing themselves on her. She was grateful for their existence, but why couldn't they exist far from her?

'Hi, Viv.'

It was the usual bunch of women all full of love, all willing to help her, and in some ways she was quite sick of it, sick of their interference, their persistence, the taking over of her life and her dreams.

'So what am I doing here this time?' she asked.

'Whatever you like, dear,' said one, with a voice and an accent Viv didn't recognise. It was the blonde woman, staring her in the face.

'I didn't ask to come here,' she continued.

'Oh, you did, Viv. Perhaps you never knew, but you still asked.'

Viv was surrounded by it, surrounded by caring and concern. It intruded; there was too much of it.

Jackie and Sheila were there, holding hands.

'Here's a bunch of flowers, Viv,' they said smiling. 'Keep them watered, arrange them nicely in a vase, and you'll have many happy hours from them.'

'I will?' asked Viv.

'Oh, yes,' said Sheila. 'You really, really will.' She kissed Viv. Her lip print, as though in very heavy lipstick, embedded itself on Viv's cheek.

'We'll take good care of you,' someone said. And Viv thought, but that's an ad, isn't it? For an airline.

She was only faintly aware of waking up and being in the world. Sheila's lipstick mark remained. Viv's hand on her cheek could feel nothing, but when she took her hand away, the lipstick feeling returned.

'So that's what it's all about,' she thought dreamily, and she seemed to be floating on the bed, as though she was part of the atmosphere. It was a feeling of utmost beauty. A few flashes of it's-none-of-their-business and why-don't-they-keep-the-hell-out remained, but floated away again. Warm as Viv was under the duvet, she could feel cold air on her face. It was the window she had left open, and a tremor went through her as she realised that they could have got into the room through that window. Perhaps they didn't know where she was after all. In any case, she figured, the opening was too small. Ah well, she thought, enjoying the contrast between the warmth and the cold, I shall leave it as it is and go back to sleep.

As soon as John had returned to Lewisham and handed Viv over to Jackie's care he headed back home. Now, waiting at the fourth or fifth set of traffic lights, tapping away impatiently on the steering wheel, he noticed a stunning red-headed woman cross the road. Her looks were the first attraction: the elegance, her hair floating in the breeze. For a few moments, he wondered where he had seen her before. Yes, that was it: she was the women with whom he had seen Ray; the woman of his dreams.

He panicked. He had to follow her, had to see her, find out whatever he had to find out, for there was something. He got out of the car to shout, did in fact shout, 'Hey, there.' No, that was not the way. It might frighten her off, but she had not reacted to his shout. Why should she? He did not know her name, could not remember what Viv had called her (if it was the same woman), except that he thought it implausible. He was just a man who could be shouting at anyone. He got back into the car, and turned the corner; it was on his route anyway.

As he parked, he watched her go towards another woman, and his heart nearly stopped. His eyesight was surely not to be doubted? A blonde woman, slightly plump, young, surely that was Pauline? Was it Pauline: it was a depiction of Pauline, Pauline near as dammit. He was certain he was going to be sick at any moment. 'Pauline, Pauline,' he yelled as he crossed the road. The cars parted as if to aid him. 'Come back, come back,' he yelled at them as they began walking slowly, seemingly with no interest in him whatsoever.

'Oh, Pauline, come back,' he yelled, desperate, hoarse. And yet he was not sure it was Pauline, was not sure of anything. There had to be a way of making her stop. Why was she with that woman, what were they doing together? That was the reason, and he had to find out. He was clawing at the air to help him, begging everything he could call upon to help him get them. He must get them.

'Come back, wait,' he yelled finally, as they passed into a shopping arcade.

He never knew how slowly he could run. It was like one

of those dreams where each step is measured against the pressure of every one before.

As he turned the corner, he could see into the shopping arcade; there were few people and none of them was right. Desperation choked him, rose in him as bitterly as if the very juices of his stomach were coming up to mock him. He threw open the glass doors and frantically, hopping from one foot to another, looked into the interiors of each shop. They were not there: not in the acrid-smelling trendy hairdressers; in the health-food shop; in the toy shop. They could not be in the shops which were boarded up, and they were not in the ones which had opened.

'Did you see two women,' he began, thrusting open the door of the bakers, and addressing the woman inside. She shifted herself from one foot to another before replying.

'Which two women?'

'Two women just now. Oh, it doesn't matter.'

He ran out again, racing back and forth, looking everywhere. But there was nowhere to look. He leaned against the wall, panting. Perhaps they had gone outside, had slipped past him. He looked into the street, went outside, and glanced up and down. There was no clue; the street was exactly as it was before. There was nothing; nothing at all.

As John reached his car, he leaned back against it, and surveyed his surroundings. He searched with his eyes every nook and cranny, every window ledge, every doorway, the hedges and bus stops. But they were nowhere, nowhere. How could they be? They had come from thin air, and that was where they had returned. As he thumped the steering wheel, John asked himself for the last of many times what he had done to deserve this.

THE PAST

One night, after she had finished the washing-up, when Pauline was out (who knew where?) with Ray, and Viv was at the youth club, Harriet said to John: 'I'm leaving you.'

She said it calmly, but there was no question that it was the end. She meant it all right. His answer was similar: 'Fair enough. I'd like to see how you get along on your own.'

He returned to the paper he had been reading, and she turned her attention to something on the television. It was nothing interesting.

'Our marriage is a mere apology for one,' she continued.

'I agree,' said John. 'but do we have to talk about it? You've decided, and that's that.'

'Have you nothing to say about a way of life which is going to end?'

'Just that you'll soon find out how hard life is outside of here.'

'Don't you think I have any idea?'

'No.'

He went back to his paper. It had been thus for such a long time, neither of them could remember a time when they had been close, although a closeness of sorts had obviously been there once upon a time. She sat staring, once again, at the TV.

'Good night,' she said frostily after a short while.

Upstairs, alone, Harriet threw herself on the bed and sobbed. She had wished for some time that one or both of them had been more inclined to do a bit of plate throwing, but no. Neither one of them was inclined to express emotion, and their idea of a failed marriage was the complete breakdown in communication which characterised their own. This was what she wanted: an end to it. Nevertheless, it was hard. The girls were old enough to look after themselves – more of less. But they would no doubt find it difficult to forgive her.

178

She came downstairs in the morning to find that John had caught the girls on their way to school and work.

'I've told them,' he said.

'You've what?'

'I said you're leaving us.'

'Just like that, no explanation, no chance for me to say anything, no attempt at a united front so that they suffer as little as possible.'

Harriet got up and walked around the room.

'You bastard,' she said. 'They're going to think the worst of me and the best of you, of course. You've made sure of that.'

'I don't think I'm a particularly good father in their terms,' he said measuredly.

'Or in mine either, or in mine.'

'When, of course, you're the greatest and most wonderful mother ever to bear children.'

Harriet went to put the kettle on for herself. She was shaking; her knees trembled. The bastard. And, of course, there was nothing on earth that she could do. They would hate her for ever.

'I don't know how you could treat them with such disrespect. Don't you care for them at all?' she said eventually. Her voice was weak.

'How soon are you going?' he said as he got up to go to work.

She and Marjorie took months to decide exactly what to do and, once they'd decided, it took further months to work out quite how to achieve it. Their friendship was new and, likewise, their thoughts of a fresh life were also exciting. But in other ways, in all other ways, Harriet looked back on this period as being the worst time in her life. Pauline and Viv seemed not at all surprised, but they were colder than ever. They had always been cold to her, cold to everyone, but she seemed to be singled out for more coldness than everyone else. One day Pauline, glowing from every pore, sat down in the front room with Ray, who looked smug.

'Ray and I are engaged,' she announced.

Harriet had difficulty remaining standing. She knew that

teenage girls did this sort of thing; that long, frequently-broken engagements were part and parcel of teenage existence, but this looked horrifically serious.

'Aren't you a bit young?' she said faintly.

'Old enough to know our own minds,' said Pauline, glancing smilingy at Ray who returned her look.

'Well, congratulations,' she whispered, not knowing what else to say.

'We were thinking of getting married this time next year, if that's all right with you,' said Ray.

'What does Dad say?' asked Harriet.

Both Pauline and Ray smiled.

'He thinks I'm too young, but he said that if that's what I really want, and I'm quite sure, then next June it shall be!'

She ended the sentence on a high note, as a triumph.

'Isn't it a bit soon?' Harriet queried.

'It's what we both want, Mum,' said Pauline gently. 'Anyway, I'll be eighteen by then.'

Harriet smiled: she hoped it looked sincere. She wasn't quite sure what was the right stance to take. Ray was a louse, she was absolutely certain of that. A complete louse, and a horrible person. He looked like a sadist. I can't allow my daughter to be married to a sadist, she thought. But she did allow it. Any dig at Ray, however slight, was matched by Pauline's hundred-times-greater defence.

Harriet moved out about three months before the wedding, on condition that the house wasn't sold until they felt Viv was ready to live on her own. Emotionally, she wanted out as soon as possible. She wanted to leave the past well behind, and she wanted the burden of her moping husband gone, too.

Viv stared at the world around her. It was as though she was surrounded by a fence. She sniffed at her arm: soapy roses hit her, one of the smells of her father's house. She wanted to capture it, to put it in a bottle she could uncork. But as she smelt it, it disappeared. It was gone.

She stared out of the window, and in her imagination could see Pauline clawing at the window, the glass panes resistant to her fingernails, scratching as they slid down the surface. It was horrible, horrible. Visions of her possible whereabouts floated across Viv's train of thought: earthy, watery, airy and fiery graves; hotel bedrooms; cellars; cupboards; hideouts amongst the bushes. She rejected all of them.

The familiar stirrings of anger began. As tiny children, she and her sister had been positively lovey-dovey. But even before Pauline hit teenage, they began to hiss and spit at each other.

Viv turned over in her bed and rested on her stomach. Her chin was in her hands, as though she were a child watching TV.

A glimpse: they were together, playing ball, laughing and shrieking and giggling. They were in their back garden, a small space, but in their imagination it was a prairie. And another: the two of them were walking along the road, hand in hand, to return their library books. A red car meant they'd see a bear, and they saw two red cars, both together. They ran and ran from the bears, convinced that if they turned around, then they'd be eaten.

Another, stronger, memory came to the fore. When Viv was about twelve, and Pauline fourteen, they were in the midst of their many rows period. They could hardly talk civilly to each other. There was one particular occasion – more extreme than usual – when she had borrowed one of Pauline's records. Pauline had come to grab it back and had grabbed so abruptly that Viv's nails had dragged across the surface, rendering it completely unplayable. Pauline had demanded that Viv buy her another one: Viv had refused.

It came back vividly now, even the way the house was decorated, newly done in wallpaper with pale purple concentric circles and shiny furniture of cheapish wood. But they had a glass coffee table that they had bought at the Ideal

181

Home exhibition. In their bedroom, squashed as it was, there was really no room to fight. The beds got in the way, and if someone fell, there was always something to fall against: the dressing-table: the record player on its little table; the walls. They both hated it, but their house was three-bedroom in name only, and the third room had space for a desk and nothing else. So everything they felt was magnified. Thus it was that day when they had the tremendous row.

It went along the lines of:

'I wish you were dead, why don't you get out?'

'I'll tell on you, you spiteful cow. Mum and Dad have got to be made to see what you're up to. You're trying to ruin my life.'

'You've ruined my life already.'

'You. You're a piddling little kid, you can't have your life ruined.'

'You're a cretin,' said Viv, making a grab for Pauline.

'You don't even know what it means,' said Pauline, ducking down by the bed, reaching out to scratch Viv's leg.

They scrabbled around in a small space for what seemed to be a long time: eventually, Pauline grabbed Viv's head, smashing it down on the floor time and again.

'I hate you,' said Viv breathlessly. Pauline just puffed and carried on her gruesome task.

'I hope your teeth fall out, your eyes rot, and you die a horrible death.' Pauline said this coldly, and she stopped hitting Viv's head. She had not done it hard enough to cause real damage, but it felt painful.

'I bet you've given me concussion,' said Viv weakly.

'You couldn't even spell it.'

Viv got up and staggered towards the stairs. She did not really mean to stagger, but it was quite easy, and anyway she didn't feel that good.

She got to the top of the stairs, and began to feel faint. Something was swimming about; the bottom of the stairs seemed to recede and come closer, get bigger and smaller, as she was watching it. Then it came yet closer to her, and everything else disappeared.

A thud, thud, thud sent Pauline rushing to the top of the

stairs, and Harriet running in from the living room. Viv was at the bottom of the stairs, sprawled out flat on her back, groaning ever more loudly.

'Oh,' shouted Pauline. 'Oh!' And she clapped her hand over her mouth, and with the other leaned against the wall. 'She's dead!'

'Don't be ridiculous,' said Harriet. 'She's making a noise: how can she be dead?'

Harriet stroked Viv's forehead, felt her pulse, and then said: 'You sit here with her; I'll call the ambulance.'

Pauline sat and sobbed; Viv opened her eyes slightly, and looked at her.

'I forgive you,' she said faintly.

Pauline sat, clutching her knees, soaking them with tears. Harriet returned, and stroked Pauline's hair as well as Viv's.

'The ambulance will be here in a minute,' she said. 'Were you two having a fight?'

Pauline nodded, creasing her lips together.

'Don't worry, I don't think there's much wrong with her.' Viv moaned again slightly, and whispered: 'My back hurts.'

Harriet again held her hand, worried, and thoughts passed through her mind like: if you break your back would it still hurt and does that mean you can never walk again?

She was moved very gently into the ambulance, and kept in overnight for X-rays and observation. Her back was painfully bruised, but there was to be no lasting damage. Pauline suffered some of the most lasting damage: she cried all night, and had nightmares for months afterwards. Viv was in bed for weeks, and every night Pauline could sense her presence in the next bed, sometimes wincing with pain.

If Viv felt any vengefulness, it would have been more than repaid by Pauline's remorse. The girl was a mass of guilt. Neither of them talked about it, but Viv gave her to understand that she was forgiven, even that she had quite forgotten about it. Pauline had not. And for the weeks until she went back to school, Viv reminded Pauline of the possibilities of power.

THE PRESENT

After a while, Jackie came in to see Viv. She was not surprised to find her buried deep beneath the covers, staring up with a puzzled expression.

'Can I get you anything?'

'Nothing I can think of for the moment.'

Jackie turned to go, but something turned her back to face Viv.

'What's this really all about, Viv?'

Viv blinked several times, looking like a frightened animal. 'I don't know.'

She reached out to take Jackie's hand. Like Marguerite's, it felt tremendously soft, but it had more life in it.

'Who do you love?'

'Somebody, nobody, you, who knows?' whispered Viv.

'Do they care for you?'

'I don't know.'

Jackie had always been bemused by Viv, even before she became ill. Viv was a mysterious woman, enigmatic. In some ways, she would not have been surprised if Viv had killed Ray, although she had not mentioned that to anyone else, and was sure the thought was cruel. But to look at Viv was to look at a shell of a person: so little of her was betrayed from the outside. She had a suspicion Viv was jealous of her relationship with Sheila – but only because of what Sheila had said of their past. As for the present, Viv reacted strangely to them, but no more strangely than she did to everyone else.

'Are your parents coming to take you away again?'

'Yes, later.'

'Didn't you want to stay with them all day?'

'They didn't ask me to.'

Jackie barely hid her annoyance. It was just imaginable that Viv was their flesh and blood. Just. But they kept dumping her at the house, not looking after her properly.

'I don't want to be a burden,' Viv whispered.

184

'Oh, Viv, you're not a burden, whatever gave you that idea?'

'Nothing.'

'It's just that, sometimes, well, we all worry about you. I know your parents do, too. And maybe now it would be better for you to go into hospital. I didn't think so to start with, but perhaps it's for the best.'

'I'm not that ill,' said Viv.

Jackie was reminded of the creepy feeling she got when Viv handed her back her own handkerchief. She was certain that she had not brought it from her own house, so where did it come from? There had to be an explanation, but she had not yet been able to think of one.

'Really, I'm OK.'

There was the sound of the key in the door, and Sheila's voice shouting hello. Jackie matched it.

'Shall we sit with you?' she asked.

'No, better not.'

'Whatever,' Jackie said.

Jackie shut the door behind her, with a feeling of relief. Viv, on the other hand, felt a gnawing in her stomach. People were all the time reaching their hands out to her, but she could not take them. Just now, she had taken Jackie's hand, but in her heart she could not accept it. And there was an uncomfortable feeling of betrayal in the air. Viv went back into herself, into an awake-sleep.

Harriet and Marjorie had a fruitless day searching the streets around Victoria. Traces of Pauline seemed obliterated, and they had no clue where else to turn. Marjorie still felt that she was right, and had seen Pauline in the pub.

Harriet greatly valued Marjorie's optimism, even if she didn't always give it credit. But she feared it was a feeble thing, always on the lookout for reasons to withdraw. At present, she could not have tolerated its disappearance.

'Can you see me ever having been with John?' Harriet asked on the train back to Eltham.

Marjorie pursed her lips: 'No, not really. It was something I'd always wondered about at the time, when you were divorcing him. He sounded so pompous. It was no wonder you kept us apart.'

'But when we first met, he was so needy. Like a lost little boy.'

'And presumably he found himself when he married you.'

'Yes,' Harriet sighed.

'Whereas you lost yourself.'

'Oh no, that's not true. I mean, I had never discovered there was a me to be found in the first place.'

'Sounds familiar.'

When they got off the train, John was there to welcome them with the car.

'No luck?' he asked.

'None whatsoever,' said Marjorie, pre-empting what she felt sure would be his scathing comments.

'Ah, well,' said John. He drove in silence. He had been wondering all day what to say about his possible sighting of Pauline. He wasn't sure whether he had made it all up, that was the trouble. Was that really Pauline he had seen? He could scarcely remember what Pauline looked like.

'I thought I saw her today,' said John after about a mile. 'I chased after her, but it was no good. Now I don't think it was her at all.'

'Oh dear,' said Marjorie sympathetically.

'I rang the police, also. They gave me the brush-off.'

'Shouldn't they be calling us in for questioning or something?'

'I suppose so,' said John. 'But they're certainly taking their time about it.'

'Maybe that just means that they don't suspect her of anything.'

'Who knows?'

There was little conversation over dinner; they had said it

all. Viv's refusal to come round stung a little, but they took nothing she said very seriously. In any event, she was going to be collected in the morning, and would not be allowed back.

John took another route to fetch Viv from her house. He was sure that the way he had gone before was not the best, and also he wanted time to be on his own before he got there. He drove to a park nearby and stared at the lake for a few moments. He was soothed by the water, and he felt at peace amongst all the other people who were quite intent on their own lives. He could go now, and be ready to collect Viv.

As he drove around the corner, he became increasingly aware of the familiarity of the place. Something was troubling him: he did not remember coming here before, and yet he must have, because the picture of it was now crystal clear. Then, with a shock so great that he jammed on the brakes and stopped the car without even bothering to see if anyone was behind him, he realised how he knew this street. It was a lonely street, one of worn-out, disused, industrial buildings, some of which were covered with corrugated iron. He was suddenly sure that if he turned the corner, he would see . . . he would see a corrugated iron fence, which had been forced open enough to let in a single body, if that body was supple and strong. And there, in the middle of the waste ground, would be a hand sticking out of the dirt.

He could not move. The car was not properly parked, it stood too far from the pavement. But there was little traffic coming through: John was not sure whether to be pelased about that or not. But he could not move. He had been literally glued to his seat. He could feel the stickiness adhering to his trousers. He was back there, back in the dream, with the greyness of the sky, the atmosphere of fore-

187

boding, and the feeling that he was in a drama of somebody else's making. Someone was directing him, and he didn't like it at all. What was he meant to do? In a way, he felt that if he did what he was meant to do, then everything would work out for the best. But for the meantime, his hands, still resting on the steering wheel, were sweating so much that little droplets were falling onto his lap. He had to act.

He drove around the corner as carefully as if he'd never driven a car before. And it was there. He approached it slowly, slowly, knowing that there was no chance anyone else would drive past. He was alone, as alone as if he was the only person still alive in the world. Then, he stayed in the car looking at the corrugated iron, wondering if he should force it, whether he was meant to force it, so that he could get inside the compound for himself. The time ticked by: he had no concept of why he was waiting there, or of how long he had stayed. But he was fixed there firmly, could not have gone anywhere even if he had wanted.

At last the time was right, and he ran, as fast as he could, as if he was being chased by thousands of monsters, towards the iron fence. John rattled it, pulled and pushed at it, trying to force himself inside. At last, at last, he pushed himself through the narrow opening.

Once in, he stared across at the ground, almost a moon-scape, with a few dirty little weeds sticking up here and there, covered in dust. It seemed so deserted, but as though it had fallen into recent disrepair, and was once a hive of something or other, some fairly unpleasant manufacturing industry, perhaps, or a depot, or warehouse.

And that was the spot. He knew it, recognised it, even though there was no sign to mark it. It was there all right. He crouched down, forgetting his clothes, forgetting that he was not able to crouch any more, forgetting everything except that he had to see what was underneath. He began to scrabble. There was nothing with which to dig; he cupped his hands and began digging in the earth, not knowing whether he would find a hand, a body, what. All around he could feel the presence of someone or something. I'm being watched, I'm being watched, he thought. But still he had to

188

continue, on and on and on, until he reached it. It was desperation, he was going to die, something would happen, but he must find out, he must find out, what was buried underneath. And he would.

Eventually, when his hands were bleeding and he was covered almost entirely with the horrible dusty dirt of the place, he hit upon something. At first, he couldn't decide what it could be. But as he cleared the dirt off the top, discovering a plastic sheet, he felt something hard and rectangular, and could breathe again. At least it wasn't a body.

Further pushing aside of the dirt showed him that, in fact, it was a briefcase. He pulled it out, and the piles of earth which formed each side of the hole fell into the centre. But he had his prize. It lay there on the ground in front of him, a maroon case swathed in thick, clear plastic. Perhaps that was what the hand had been telling him in his dreams: dig here. He caressed the plastic, brushing the fragments of dirt from the crevices of the folded cover. And finally he pulled out the briefcase. It was fine leather, very smooth to touch, but no longer smelling of leather, rather of earth, as though it and the earth had become one.

The lock, dammit it, was a combination, but he twisted and turned and somehow, by some fluke, the lock clicked, and there: it was open. His blood ran cold. Inside, packed so that no more could possibly be put in, was money: fivers, tenners, he could not guess how much. All in little bundles with bank wrappers on them noting the quantity. He did not want to know. So he was waiting here with the proceeds of a robbery? What was it? Did that woman put it here, or did Ray? He didn't know, but he had to get rid of it as quickly as possible. Not here, not here, but somewhere.

He jumped to his feet, and discovered he was very stiff, because he had been crouched down for God knows how many hours. Also he was filthy, but that didn't matter, not compared to the discovery he had made, and the decisions he now had to take. He left the plastic where it lay, and, twisting the combinations on the lock, took the briefcase and walked awkwardly towards the fence.

189

It was difficult to get out, although not quite as difficult as it had been to get in. As he finally emerged from the compound, he noticed two men coming towards him. They bore a striking dissimilarity to him: to start with, they were both immaculately dressed. This made John ashamed, as though he had been caught doing something lavatorial. But although he had no idea who they were, he expected them there, knew that whatever it was they were going to do was what happened next.

'Good afternoon,' said the elder one warmly. His coat, a light, pale one, was resting on his shoulders.

'Allow me to relieve you of that.'

There was no one about, no car in which they could have arrived. Nothing. And John gave them the case with relief, immeasurably glad that he no longer had the burden of it. Besides, he felt sure it belonged to them morally anyway. The two men bowed slightly to him, their faces expressionless. Then they turned and began to walk in the direction from which they had come. John stood by his car and watched them. Eventually, they disappeared, became small dots which merged with the horizon.

He got into his car, and turned it round as quickly as he could. He wanted to go, anywhere that would not lead him to the men, to be off as far and as quickly as possible from this place, and never to set foot in it again. He had done his job, and now should be left in peace.

Although she was still sunk down with betrayal, Viv was slowly roused by the tinkling noise of small pebbles being thrown at her window. Some of them came through the open fanlight and landed just inside on the floorboards. Her first impulse was to run to the window and look. Outside, gazing up at her, was Marguerite Dumas, her brilliant hair and wonderful clothes a stunning contrast to the greyness of the sky.

'I have something to say to you. May I come in?'

She was smiling, and Viv could not say no. She went downstairs to open the door, hoping that no one would hear her. They walked up the stairs in silence, and Viv, for the first time in a while, felt her room was untidy, and that she should not have people looking at it in this state. Marguerite perched on a chair arm, one foot tucked behind the other.

'My sister and I would like to thank you,' she smiled. 'You've helped us very much. My cousins, too, are grateful.'

She bent down and kissed Viv, who smelt the scent of someone who is never dirty, who would bathe so often that their own personal identification would be washed away. She smelt like a hyacinth, or something. It was horrible.

'I don't know what you mean,' said Viv.

'You don't need to.'

She smiled at Viv once again, and shut the door.

I saw an angel, a plastic one, come into my room and try to placate me. Now I no longer know what to believe. And in any case, I don't know her sister. Now my father comes into my room; he's been rolling around in the dirt. That must have been what he's been doing for all that time since they rang up and said he's coming to pick you up and I said no, don't bother. I thought he'd changed his mind, that they'd decided to let me alone, do what I wanted for a change. And he says to me not to worry, that there's nothing to worry about any more. But I don't understand: how can he know what I've been worrying about? Does he get inside my head or something, open a little part of me and climb in, the way I used to feel he did way back? Now they're all in my room, all the people from this house, and they're telling me to go with him, that it would be the best for everyone. And I think, yes, they're right, it would be the best. But I wish they wanted me here, because here I'm so much safer than I was with my parents. Eric and Sheila, and, of course, Jackie, Jackie who I know is annoyed, exasperated with me, but who comes into my dreams, helps me anyway (what do I do for her?). They are safer than my father, who tells me that I haven't got anything to worry about. How can he tell? I bet he's never wondered if he's killed anyone.

They are all standing around me in a semi-circle, and I long to touch them, long to accept whatever it is that they're offering. Perhaps it is nothing, but I can feel it as surely as if they were touching me. But I'm still lying on the bed, in my messed-up heap of a duvet, motionless.

Just then, there's a knock on the door and a sudden hush. As if in slow motion, the door opens and falls back to the wall. We all turn to look at it.

'The front door was open and I just walked in,' the voice said apologetically.

And it was Pauline, leaning against the doorframe, looking a hollow version of herself.

Pauline slumped in a chair as everyone stared at her.

'Well,' she said after a while, 'isn't anyone going to tell me they're pleased to see me?'

No one moved.

'Please,' she said.

'I'm going to ring your mother,' said John crossly. He went downstairs leaving behind him an air of anger, of discomfort. Viv dragged herself from the bed; the other three wondered if it might not be more politic to get out, but were curious none the less.

'Where the hell have you been?' asked Viv.

Pauline shrugged: 'Around.'

'Around!' Viv spat. 'And you came back to me and let

everyone think I was going out of my mind when I said you'd come to see me. But it was you, it was, and now they'd bloody well better believe it.'

Pauline frowned:

'Well, we spoke on the phone ... and I did come to see you ... but I didn't know where your room was. I couldn't face ... I just had to go.'

John returned:

'I'm taking the two of you over to my house and no arguing.'

'Don't you think you ought to ask us if that's what we want?' said Viv angrily.

'No. I think it's about time you took notice of us for a change, even if you are such bloody grown-ups, in charge of your own lives.'

'You want us to be under your jurisdiction again, don't you, to deny us ourselves? I want to stay here.'

'Oh, come on,' said Pauline. 'Let's just go.'

She sounded very tired. Viv stood up, stepped into her clothes. 'All right then, come on.' She'd had enough of arguing. She hugged Eric, Sheila and Jackie, one after the other, as though she'd never see them again. She felt the softness and the firmness of them; their sizes and their individualities. All three looked at her with relief.

The Fosters went downstairs and got into the car, Viv without belongings, Pauline clutching her shoulder bag.

'The police let me go, but they're going to have me in again for questioning before the inquest.'

There was no reply; tears were streaming down John's face.

'Well, aren't you glad to see me?'

Viv sighed. John said: 'Yes, of course we're glad.'

They travelled along some more in the darkness.

'I've never been this way before,' said Viv.

They pulled up outside the house to see the three women waiting there for them.

'So, you're still alive,' said Harriet beginning to cry. Pauline began to cry, too; eventually, she became so hysterical, she had to be helped into a chair.

'It's such a relief,' she sighed eventually. 'I couldn't take it much longer.'

'So tell us,' Viv cried. 'What happened? For God's sake, tell us.'

'Yes. Just hold on. Please!' Pauline looked down at her lap, steadied herself before she began. It came out with force.

'He persecuted me, he went on and on at me, how I wasn't a good wife, and he hated me. I could have hated him, it was so terrible, my life and what he was doing to me. He never spoke a civil word, not for years, and as for affection, well, you can forget it. The only thing half-nice he would do was sometimes throw himself at my feet and beg forgiveness.'

She took a breath.

'I didn't do it, I couldn't kill anyone. But he said, well, he said they'd all think it was me. I don't know what I did to him, why he hated me so much. Then he said that he didn't deserve me, that I would leave him eventually because no one could love him as he was. I thought it would be me that he'd do in, but he never went that far.' She became bitter; stopped for a moment and scratched her jeans. 'No, he just confined himself to knocking me about. The swine.'

She started to cry once more, tears trickling down her cheeks and then through her fingers as she pressed them against her cheeks.

'So now I've been hiding, but it didn't last very long, did it? I gave myself up. After you' (she pointed at Marjorie) 'came up to me in the pub, I thought: they'll get me. I can't go on like this for the rest of my life, running away with no money and not the least idea of how to get away. Away from everyone. So I turned myself in to the police.' Loathing, despair and self-loathing crossed her face.

'I don't understand: why did you have to run away?' asked Viv. 'And why did you come back?'

'I couldn't bear to be all alone, without anyone or anything, worried; worried all the time that I'd be caught. He said it was my fault he was going to do it, and it was me they'd think had done it. He sat in a chair in the bedroom calmly telling me all this, and as he stuck the knife into

194

himself, he wrapped a handkerchief around it so he wouldn't leave fingerprints. He thrust it hard, hard . . .'

She was choking, and had to rest for a few moments before continuing.

'He stabbed himself and blood started to go onto the floor, into a pool. It was horrible. And there was nothing I could do. I stood and watched him. He had the most ghastly expression on his face. He was just looking at me, as though he was feeling nothing, nothing at all. Then I tried to grab his hand, and the knife. But when he moved, blood went all over the place, and my hand got cut, too. I tried to stop him, don't you see? I tried to stop him, but there was nothing I could do. He was stronger than me, even when he was bleeding to death. And he said if I called an ambulance, he'd tell the ambulancemen that I'd done it, that I'd tried to kill him, and I was covered in blood, his blood. Of course, they'd believe him, he was right, they'd believe him and not me.'

Pauline was exhausted, had exhausted everyone.

'That's not true, Pauline,' said Viv eventually. 'You are strong. You're here, after all, and you've won. He's dead, yes, but you're alive and we all know, and the police know, that it's not your fault. Ray was wrong: you're the one we believe.'

And with tears covering her own face, Viv put her arms around Pauline, something she had not done since childhood. Pauline was alive and innocent and she, so was she.

THE FUTURE

I live very high up now, in a tower block, and I can see all over London. I've got that mirror up in my room, the same one I had in Lewisham. God knows where it came from initially.

Whereas then the truth from the mirror was distorted, now it's true, quite true. Before; yes, I was mad, I admit it now. Or rather my perceptions of reality were diminished. Now I see reality for what it is.

It was three years ago, all that stuff, three long and fairly packed years – for me, at any rate. Not for Harriet and Marjorie, or John and Penny, although they might have quite different stories. I've been healing myself, that's what I've been doing. And so, of course, I know that I'm all right, that what I thought was my madness was sensitivity and a gift, a supreme gift.

Jackie and Sheila still love each other. Jackie's training to be an accountant, not something I'd have expected, and Sheila's a local councillor. I see them – sometimes – and Jackie now lives in my old room. Eric has opened a restaurant in Paris, a vegetarian restaurant. I find that very hard to believe, I mean, he always liked cooking, but it's not what I'd have thought he would do for a living. People always confound your expectations.

I suppose I've confounded everybody. I'm two years into my training as an acupuncturist. I'll be getting quite a lot of money, I expect, depending on the number of people I see. And I see more people now, of course, have more friends, even if I'm not yet up to having a lover.

But it's Pauline who most confounds me. She marries a maniac who kills himself and tries to blame her. Now what does she do but get married all over again. Brian is OK, I suppose. They seem to get on well. Seem to. She got married in cream, and carried this great big bunch of flowers. And she's not even pregnant. There really is no excuse.

Mum wouldn't come. She said Pauline was throwing her

196

life away, and she wasn't going to be a spectator this time, even if Brian did seem to be all right. Pauline didn't look as though she minded too much. Dad was there, and Penny. But, of course, he really believes in marriage, thinks he and Penny set a good example. But I agree with Mum.

I don't know why I went, really.